T0279068

PRAISE FOR *AFTER LIFE*

"Gayle Forman has an uncanny ability to create characters in which we see ourselves, and her latest—which looks at where love goes, after a loss—is an honest, heartbreaking elegy to how memory makes relationships eternal."

—JODI PICOULT, #1 *New York Times* bestselling author

"*After Life* is a beautifully woven, extraordinary page-turner about a girl who has miraculously come back to life. But is it actually a miracle? I was consumed by this thought-provoking, deftly written, multilayered novel. Gayle Forman reigns as the queen of breaking hearts with a touch of magic."

—ADAM SILVERA, #1 *New York Times* bestselling author of *They Both Die at the End*

"Forman is a master at making her readers fall in love—with a girl whose life is over, with a community of people in a small town who are barely surviving her loss, and with the incredible, surprising way everyone's stories knit together into a heartbreaking and hopeful whole."

—E. LOCKHART, #1 *New York Times* bestselling author of *We Were Liars* and *Genuine Fraud*

"A masterful tale about a family coping with loss, showing the way grief affects us in ways we don't even see. Once I met Amber and her family, I didn't want to let them go."

—BRIGID KEMMERER, *New York Times* bestselling author of *Carving Shadows into Gold*

"Full of grace and beauty, this book asks big questions about loss and grief, guilt and forgiveness, without ever straying from its true center: the unbreakable bond of sibling love. Forman weaves seemingly unconnected threads throughout the book, blurring the lines between fate and coincidence, until bringing it all together in a revelatory ending."

—DAVID ARNOLD, *New York Times* bestselling author of *Mosquitoland*

"I remember reading my first Gayle Forman book and how it felt like I was holding magic in my hands. *After Life* is no different. An immersive, impossible to put down story about love, loss, and most importantly, memory. A testament to the bond between sisters."

—RACHAEL LIPPINCOTT, #1 *New York Times* bestselling author of *Five Feet Apart*

After
Life

ALSO BY GAYLE FORMAN

After Life

GAYLE FORMAN

Quill Tree Books
An Imprint of HarperCollins Publishers

Quill Tree Books is an imprint of HarperCollins Publishers.

After Life
Copyright © 2025 by Gayle Forman, Inc.
Interior art © 2025 by Agata Wierzbicka
All rights reserved. Manufactured in Harrisonburg, VA,
United States of America.

Library of Congress Control Number: 2024939826
ISBN 978-0-06-334614-7

Typography by Laura Mock
24 25 26 27 28 LBC 5 4 3 2 1

First Edition

AMBER

It's always that last hill that does me in. It's so steep, so long. Up past the middle school, past McBurney Farm, past the flashing lights at the four-way stop. I have to stand in my bike's saddle to make it. My thighs burn. Even on the coldest day, I sweat. But once I reach the crest, it all feels worth it. There's this delicious moment. Picture a feather, suspended in midair, about to float to earth. The hard work of the hill, of school, behind me. Ahead of me: home.

In winter, I pedal down hard and fast. The wind bites my face, but anticipating the warmth awaiting me makes the pain almost pleasurable. On milder days, in spring or early fall, when the afternoon sun oozes like honey, I take my time, coasting down, arms at my sides. On those days, the wind sometimes feels like it might lift me up right out of the seat, like I could fly the rest of the way home.

When I reach the summit today, my thighs don't burn. Not

even a little. Going up felt like going on the flat. Maybe after nearly four years of this route to and from school every day, with only a few weeks until graduation, I'm finally used to it.

On the way down, I lift my hands to my sides, whipping past the church, past the Circle K, past the car wash, past someone's white ten-speed bike chained to a lamppost. I don't have my helmet on, so my hair flies behind me like a superhero cape.

I round the corner onto our block. I don't see Mom's car in the driveway, which maybe means she's out with Missy, at youth group or therapy or whatever the latest thing is they're making Missy go to because she's a weirdo who has no friends. If the house is empty, Calvin can come over, unless he has work or wrestling practice. I can't remember what he told me in p.m. homeroom. I also can't remember if Missy has something today, and usually I keep track of that so I know when I can sneak Calvin in. What day does she have youth group again? What day is it, even? It's strange that I can't remember, considering I've spent the last seven periods writing the date on the heading of various notes, quizzes, and assignments.

At the last graduation assembly, our principal, Mrs. Wu, warned us against senioritis. She said it typically afflicts students after they get their college acceptances. They blow off homework, ditch class, oversleep, forget their own names. "Because you sense the end is coming," she said. "But it's not here yet, so while it's okay to loosen the grip, don't let go until the ink on your diploma is dry."

Mom always leaves the garage door open for me, but today it's down and locked. There's been a spate of break-ins, so I guess we're being security conscious. Nice of someone to tell me.

I park my bike next to the gate and hop the back fence. The patio door is also locked, but there's a spare key carved into the false bottom of a papier-mâché rock that Missy made. This is what she does—crafts hiding spots, writes elaborate notes in code. She wants to be a spy when she grows up, like it's a legit career option. And Mom wonders why she has no friends.

"Anyone home?" I call as I nudge open the door. The house feels not just quiet, but uninhabited, like Aunt Pauline's place when she's out of town for months on end and we go to collect her mail. Not even Mr. Fluff comes out to bunt against my legs.

It's also freezing in here. I pad across the living room to the thermostat. It reads sixty-eight degrees, which is what Mom leaves it at when no one's home. But the house feels like a meat locker, the way it got when the furnace went on the blink last winter and we all had to sleep in the living room, with space heaters and the fireplace going all night. I can hear the heater ticking, see the air blowing against Mom's knitting supplies. I shiver. I better not be getting sick! I go to grab an afghan from the front-hall closet, but the shelf where Mom keeps all her crocheted blankets has nothing but Mr. Fluff's cat bed—I guess Mom got him a new one— and a bunch of moving boxes labeled *Amber*. How very on-brand of Mom to get a jump on college packing before I've even graduated. There are no blankets, so I grab a random gray hoodie that's hanging next to Mom's old trench coat and flop down onto the couch. I flick on the TV to catch the last fifteen minutes of my favorite talk show, only I can't find the channel it's on—I can't find the channels, period.

Something is just off with me today. I go into the kitchen to grab the phone to call Casey like I always do after school. Only when I start to dial, I can't remember her number. Or Calvin's. Or ours. I stare at the handset and try to summon the digits, but the numbers just stare back at me, not about to give away their secrets. The harder I try to pull up the numbers, the farther away they swim. Okay. This happened once at school when I thought too hard about my locker combo. I had to close my eyes and let muscle memory take over. I put the handset to my ear, but nothing happens. There's not even a dial tone.

I shiver harder this time. The kitchen is usually the warmest room in the house because the ancient gas stove always emits heat, but it's as cold as the living room. I really hope I'm not getting sick. I put my palm against my forehead. Alexa had mono and was out of school for five weeks. I have prom coming up. And graduation. The most important weeks of my life—I cannot miss them.

When the garage door opens, I'm a little bummed because it means Mom's home and Calvin can't come over, but I'm also relieved because if I'm sick, she'll take care of me. It's what she does. I head to the door that leads from the kitchen to the garage to meet Mom, catching a glimpse of a framed photo on the wall of me in my cap and gown.

"Hey, Mom," I call before she gets out of the car. "When did the graduation portraits come in?"

She doesn't answer. I step into the garage.

From inside the car, Mom begins to scream.

NICK
Seven Years Before

Nick Flores hated his job. All his life, he had wanted to be an artist, using camera and film as his paint and canvas. He'd put himself through art school, and after graduation he got a job ostensibly as a photographer, but really he was more of a factory worker, no more an artist than the guy flipping burgers at Mickey D's.

Maybe that would be better. More honest. At least then he wouldn't be bullshitting anyone—unlike now, calling himself a photographer while shooting school pictures for the Ansel Fitch Photo Studio. What a joke. There was no Ansel Fitch. They made up the name to evoke a real photographer. It was a freaking sacrilege, if you asked Nick. Which no one did.

Ansel Fitch Photo Studio wasn't even a studio. It was an assembly-line corporation operating in twelve states that did life photos for every occasion, from preschool through graduation

5

to wedding pictures to family portraits. *From cradle to grave*, the suits joked in private, but really, if they could find a way to take photos on people's deathbeds, Nick was sure they would.

Whenever Nick tried to diverge from the Ansel Fitch template, he got in trouble. "Be creative on your own time," they told him.

As a kid, Nick had always worn a camera around his neck so he'd be ready when a shot revealed itself. He'd loved the mystery of film, never knowing what moment you would capture until you got into the darkroom. But now everything was digital, immediate, with no room left for surprises. His job was not to capture a moment but to color in an outline. And he hated it. He hated cajoling second graders to sit still. He hated bridesmaids asking one another if they looked fat. He hated graduation portraits most of all. It wasn't even the kids. The seniors at least approached the whole thing with a sense of gravitas. The same guys who made buffoons of themselves at the winter formals, cupping their balls and thrusting to prove what big men they were, stared straight into the camera when it was graduation portrait time. It was like they were trying to see their futures.

And *that* was why he hated it. These kids were on the cusp of it all, while here he was, age thirty-three, but somehow already over the dip of the hill without ever hitting the summit. It depressed the hell out of him.

He looked at his clipboard to call the next kid on his graduation portrait list. "Amber Crane."

"Right here," a girl answered. She was pretty in a generic

sort of way, a white girl, with honey-colored hair, twisted into an elaborate updo, too much eyeshadow. She was one of a million. Was that why she seemed familiar? He'd shot this school's homecoming and junior prom last year, so she'd probably gone to those. She looked like the kind of girl who went to school dances. He would probably shoot her at prom in a few weeks. Cradle to grave, like Ansel Fitch wanted.

She handed him her order form. She had chosen the sunset background. He gestured to the chair and she sat, smiling nervously. He started to take the photo but she held up her hands. "Hang on," she said. "It's my last one, so I want it to be good."

"Your last one?"

"My last school portrait," she said. "It *is* my graduation picture."

And then she smiled, and something changed. If a second ago she looked generic, now she was specific, which made her beautiful. Nick knew from experience that such moments were fleeting. He snapped the picture, hoping he'd captured it.

AMBER

My first thought is that there's a burglar behind me, someone with a knife or a gun, breaking into the house. I look over my shoulder, but the kitchen is empty. I turn back to Mom, who's sitting in the passenger seat of a car, not our minivan but some sedan I don't recognize. Maybe Aunt Pauline's? Someone else is driving, a guy with short hair. Maybe the minivan is in the shop and this is someone from the dealership giving Mom a lift home. But where is Missy? And what's wrong with Mom?

She's whimpering now, with her arms behind her head, like the brace position they show on the airline safety cards that Missy studied religiously that one time we flew to Florida. I told her that if you had to assume the brace position, chances were that you were already a goner. But Missy insisted that some people survived plane crashes and that they could be the ones who'd studied the card. "Sometimes, the line between living and dying is that small," my weirdo sister told me.

The driver opens the car and out steps not a guy, but a girl my age with very short, very blue hair. She has on pants with a wallet chain and chunky black boots.

Is she why Mom's freaking? Is Mom being carjacked?

"What did you do to my mom?" I demand.

As soon as I speak, Mom's whimpering stops. She stumbles out of the car, her knees buckling. I go to help her—maybe we're sick with the same bug?—but as I move toward her, she rears back, falling on her butt.

"Mom, what's wrong?"

The girl with the blue hair comes around and lifts Mom from under her arms, whispering something into her ear.

"Is she sick?" I ask the girl.

"I don't think so." She turns back to my mom and tells her, "It's okay. It's okay."

"It is so not okay. She's freaking out!"

"Call . . . call nine-one-one," Mom says in a choked voice.

"I'll do it," I say, but Mom isn't asking me. She's asking the blue-haired girl, who's pulled a slender phone from her pocket. She taps at the screen a few times and puts the phone to her ear. She performs this entire operation without taking her eyes off me.

I can hear the operator answer: "Nine-one-one. What is your emergency?"

The blue-haired girl is wearing a shirt with bowling pins and a name. I squint and read the lettering. It says *Carl*. Is her name Carl? She holds the phone out at Mom. "What should I tell them?"

Mom says nothing.

"Nine-one-one, what is your emergency?" the voice repeats.

The blue-haired girl looks at Mom. Who says nothing. Her face is frozen, mouth open, like that famous *Scream* painting.

"Sorry, pocket dial," the blue-haired girl says.

"What is going on?" I ask again. "Why is she like this? Who are you?"

"Amber." It jolts me to hear this stranger say my name. "It's me." She taps herself on the chest.

"Who are you?" I repeat.

"Who. Are. *You*?" Mom demands, her voice a guttural growl.

It's a spring day but the cold invades my bones like it's the dead of winter. I start to really shake now.

"What do you mean? I'm Amber. I just got home from school."

"How?" she gasps.

"How? On my bike, like always."

"*What* bike?"

"Why are you being like this? *My* bike."

I walk to where I left it and wheel it into the garage. At the sight of my bike, Mom drops to her knees again, closing her eyes. "No," she says. "This isn't real. None of this is real."

"But I see her, too," the girl says.

"It has to be some kind of hologram or something—someone's idea of a twisted joke," Mom says.

"Mom, look," the blue-haired girl says. She points to the bike's license plate. *Amber*, it reads. "Remember how Aunt Pauline said she had to special order it?" She starts to pull it off.

"Don't touch it!" Mom shrieks. "Don't touch it, Melissa."

Melissa?

It can't be. Melissa—Missy—my little sister, is nine. This girl must be around my age. "Who are you?" I ask her a third time.

The girl steps forward, her hand hovering a few inches over the bike's saddle. "I'm your sister, Amber," she says. "I'm Melissa."

"No, you're not. Melissa is nine." I pause, remembering. "About to turn ten."

"That was seven years ago." She pauses. "Seven years ago when you died."

MELISSA

Eleven Years Before

Missy knew that Auntie Pauline was getting Amber a bike for her thirteenth birthday before Amber knew. Before her parents even knew. She knew this because Missy paid attention. She had always paid attention. Even before she'd decided she wanted to be a spy when she grew up, she'd been watching, learning. It was the paying attention that made Missy want to be a spy, not the other way around.

The thing was there were signs and hints and clues everywhere, like fruit dangling from a tree. If you paid attention, it was all there for the picking.

Missy paid attention to her aunt's internet searches, so she knew that she'd found a secondhand bike that was a terrific deal because her aunt had searched for the bike new and the used one cost way less. She also knew the bike was "like new," and this would be important to Amber, who'd be embarrassed to tell her friend Casey she'd gotten something used because Casey's family was the kind that donated almost-new bikes and Amber and Missy's family was the kind that bought almost-new bikes that other people had cast off.

She knew from the argument her mom and Auntie Pauline had that her mother thought that even used and a terrific deal, this was too much money and too much bike. "She's still growing," her mom told Pauline. "Let's just wait."

She knew her aunt had enlisted her father's help when she'd seen an email printed out in the tray, with a note from her aunt to her dad: "Brian, look at the color! It's orange. Amber, you might say. Meant to be. Talk to Glo?"

She knew from the story of how her parents met how much her dad believed in meant-to-bes, particularly where bikes were concerned.

She knew that her father had agreed to help Auntie Pauline when she heard him say to her mother, "I know it's big but she'll grow into it, and it's important for Pauline to be able to do this for her."

She knew that her father had won over her mother when she'd heard her aunt special-ordering the license plate over the phone. "It should read A-M-B-E-R," she said. "Same color as the bike."

"I know what you're getting for your birthday," Missy bragged to Amber. She wasn't going to tell. A spy never told. But she wanted Amber to know that she knew.

"Is it a phone?" Amber asked. She desperately wanted the latest phone that Casey had, even though it was obvious their mother would never get her one for her thirteenth birthday, maybe not even for her eighteenth birthday.

"It's not a phone," Missy said.

This made her the bearer of bad news and the earner of her sister's ire.

"What do you know?" Amber sneered. "Get out of my room, you little creep!"

If their parents were home, Amber would have gotten a scolding for talking to Missy that way, but they weren't, so the remark went unnoticed. And anyway, as mean as Amber could be, Missy didn't really mind.

People were often what her ELA teacher, Ms. Gibbons, called "unreliable narrators," meaning they spoke one way but acted another. Her parents were reliable narrators. They said what they meant and meant what they said. But Amber was more the unreliable type. Sometimes her sister could be cruel, calling Missy a weirdo, a freak, or a creeper, slamming the door in her face, mocking her to her friends. But on the other hand, Amber would do nice things for her, like leaving a copy of *Harriet the Spy* on Missy's bed, even though she made fun of Missy for thinking herself a spy. Missy had loved the book and its sequel, which had materialized on her bed a few weeks after the original, even if she and Harriet were completely different kinds of spies. Harriet wanted the goods on other people. Missy was looking for something else. And her sister seemed to hold the key to it. She was one way and also another. This was why she fascinated Missy. She seemed to dance in two worlds.

The night of Amber's thirteenth birthday, they were going out to dinner—Amber, Missy, Mom, Dad, and Auntie Pauline, who had swapped trips with another flight attendant to be there. They were waiting outside their house for their aunt to arrive. She was often late because planes were often late. Her father stared at his watch. "The reservation is at seven," he said. "We might have to do this after."

"Do what after?" Amber asked.

Just then Missy saw her aunt, riding up their cul-de-sac, her scarf billowing behind her. "There she is!" Missy cried happily.

"Why's Pauline on a bike?" Amber asked. "Is her car busted again?"

So many secrets lived inside Missy, bursting to come out. Some of the secrets she didn't even understand. But if she kept paying attention, she knew one day she would.

Missy could contain it no longer. "It's your present!"

"Ohmygod!" Amber cried, turning to Mom and Dad. "Thank you so much!"

"Don't thank us," Mom replied. "This was Pauline's doing."

Amber was gathering Pauline in a hug before she had stopped the bike. "Thankyouthankyouthankyou!"

"You're welcome, welcome, welcome," Pauline said, laughing as she hopped off and transferred the handlebars to Amber, pointing out the little license plate affixed to the back. "I couldn't resist because the bike is amber, too! But you don't have to keep the nameplate if it's too babyish."

"It's perfect!" Amber swung her legs over the seat; even on

tippy-toes she could barely touch the ground.

Her mom winced.

"She'll be fine," Pauline said.

"It's beautiful," Missy said.

"Wanna ride it?" Pauline asked. "After Amber gets a go?"

"In your dreams," Amber snarked. "This baby's mine."

"Amber!" her parents admonished, looking worriedly at Missy for signs of envy or hurt. She understood why they thought she was jealous of Amber—who had friends and now a shiny bicycle and who Missy watched constantly—but they were wrong.

If she wanted to ride Amber's bike, it was for the same reason she sometimes tried on her clothes or sneaked peeks in her backpack to read the notes she and her friends passed during school. She wanted to understand how Amber moved through the world. This was key to something that Missy was trying so very hard to figure out.

Auntie Pauline winked at Missy just as Amber pushed off the curb. Her sister's smile was as bright as the evening sun that was starting to tilt west, its slanting beams reflecting off the bike, making it glow. She pedaled halfway up the block, stumbling a bit before righting herself.

Mom grabbed Pauline's arm. "The bike really is too big for her. She's barely five feet."

"She'll grow into it. She just needs more time," Pauline said, pulling Mom into her chest with one hand and grabbing Missy with the other. Dad went around to Mom's other side and took her hand and they all watched Amber ride into the sunset.

AMBER

I throw up in the rosebushes. Nothing comes out. No food, no liquid, no bile. It's like there's nothing in me. I blink. Mom's rosebushes are starting to bloom. She plants one for each of us, with little placards next to them with the variety of the rose and our names: Missy, Dad, Pauline, and I all have one.

"Please," I say to the blue-haired girl who is claiming to be my sister. "Tell me what's happening."

"Maybe we should go inside." She turns to Mom. "And call Dad."

Mom nods numbly.

The girl heaves Mom's arm around her shoulder and starts to walk. Mom stumbles but the girl catches her. I watch them go together, trying to figure out what the hell is going on. The blue-haired girl turns around. "Are you coming?"

I look down at the rosebushes. Mine used to be in the

middle. It was called Wildfire because of the color, a smoky orange, amber, like me. I'm standing right in front of where it used to be, only there's no flower, just dirt.

Inside, Mom is pulling a dusty bottle of whiskey from the kitchen cabinet. Aside from a Christmas toast, I've hardly seen her drink. The bottles were for guests, most of them gifts from Dad's clients.

The blue-haired girl who claims to be my sister is on her phone again. "Dad," she says. "You need to come home. To the house. Now." She pauses. "It's an emergency. No, not like that. You won't believe it unless you see it. Please come. Now."

She hangs up. I glance at the graduation photo on the wall. There's a plaque beneath it with two dates. One I recognize. One I don't.

The blue-haired girl claiming to be my sister comes up next to me. She touches one of the dates: August 8, my birthday. Then the other, April 28.

"Is this . . . ?" I ask her.

She nods.

"How?"

"You got knocked off your bike on your way home from school."

"That's insane! I'm literally standing right here. I rode home on that very bike."

Mom shoots back another glass of whiskey. The girl walks over to the secretary desk and opens a drawer, extracting a file folder. She hands it to me. *Amber*, it reads in my dad's neat block print. I open the file. Inside is a sheaf of newspaper clippings with pictures of me in them, with my family, one with Calvin.

"Here's your obituary," the girl says, handing me a small article.

Amber Marie Crane died Thursday afternoon from injuries sustained in a hit-and-run bicycle accident. She was seventeen years old.

A senior at Kennedy High School, Amber was set to graduate in the spring and attend college, where she was hoping to apply her lifelong love of musical theater to a career in teaching or music therapy.

Amber starred in frequent productions at Kennedy High School and at Sing a Song! musical summer camp, where she also worked as a counselor.

Amber is survived by her parents, Gloria and Brian Crane, her sister, Melissa, and her aunt, Pauline Clarke.

A funeral mass will be held at Church of the Holy Name Tuesday at noon followed by a wake at the family's home.

I hold the paper in my hands. It says nothing. It says exactly what I thought it would.

ARNOLD
Nine Years Before

A rnold King had been giving his sophomore ELA class the same assignment for more than two decades. It never failed to start a conversation. That was why he liked it. There had been a few principals over the years, usually the younger ones, who had not yet grown into their shoes, who questioned it. "Isn't it morbid?" they asked. One particularly foolish one had wondered if it might encourage suicide.

By now he had been doing this long enough—twenty-eight years; he was eligible for retirement but he had no interest in hanging it up just yet—to know how to handle the nervous Nellies.

"I'm not asking my students to think about their deaths," he explained. "I'm inviting them to imagine their lives."

This year's sophomore class was no different. When he announced that day's assignment was to write their own obituary, the class went through the usual stages: the laughter, the posturing and bravado, and then, as they got to work, a near universal silence.

"This is not an exercise in morbidity," he told the class as he had done each year. "Quite the opposite. I want you to envision the life you want to have lived. You can write whatever you want. Be an NBA champion or president or the first woman to walk on the moon if you want. Write whatever future you want for yourself."

"Oh, I see what you're doing," one principal had said. "You're having them manifest their dream lives." That was a very touchy-feely way of looking at it and Arnold had objected with a huffy "I most certainly am not." But he did want them to think concretely about the life they wanted to live, how it would look after they'd lived it. More than anything else he taught them—the persuasive essay, the proto–college essay, the short story, the cover letter—this felt like the most important exercise he did with his students.

After they'd completed their assignments, he invited them to share what they'd written with the class. "They say you never get to read your own obituary," he told his students. "Here's your chance."

They never ceased to surprise him. Today, for instance, Jaime Rodriguez, the shy boy who sat near the window and never spoke unless called upon, said he had had a full career as an opera singer, with very specific details about the parts he had performed. Calvin Judd, the wrestler who sat in the back and never seemed to pay attention, had some vague details about how after going to business school and "making millions" on inventions (which showed that Calvin had not fully grasped the details of how business school worked), he had come home to marry his high school sweetheart. With the way Calvin had blushed red to the ears, Arnold understood he had a specific sweetheart in mind. Next up had been Francesca Stolari, a chatty girl who was constantly passing notes and whispering to her friends, no matter how many warnings he issued. She wrote that she had opened an animal reserve in Botswana (he was surprised she even knew where that was) and had never married and never had children but had left a legacy of offspring in the animals she'd rescued.

But maybe this year's biggest surprise was Amber Crane. She was one of his most gifted writers. Lively and imaginative, she'd excelled on the more creative assignments. The one-act play she had written showed particular promise. He'd expected great things from her. When it was her turn to read her obituary, she'd come to the front of the room, the paper in her hand shaking. This was not completely unheard of. Facing mortality was hard.

"Amber Crane was born on August 8," she began in a shaky voice and then she stopped.

"Go on, Amber," he encouraged.

"That's all I have," she said. "I just couldn't think of anything more."

AMBER

In AP Psychology class, we did a unit on the human brain and Mrs. Haverford taught us about dreams. She said that dreams *feel* as if they are happening for hours, but most last only a few minutes. It's just that in sleep, time warps and wanders.

I have a recurring nightmare in which Dina Weston has come over and is knocking on the front door, but as much as I try, I can never open it. It doesn't sound like a nightmare but when I wake from it, with dread hard and solid in my veins, it feels like one.

The doorbell rings. Only in this dream, the door does open. And it's not Dina standing there—it's Dad, finger on the bell. "What's this all about?" Dream Dad asks in an uncharacteristically blustery tone.

"Just come see," the blue-haired girl claiming to be my sister says.

Dad freezes in the entryway. He looks at me and collapses to his knees. "Lord God, name above all names, your power is unlimited and your strength has no end," he prays.

At this, my mother starts to scream again.

Amber, wake up, I tell myself.

My father stands and walks toward me. This being what I've decided is a dream, I'm not sure what he'll do. Maybe he'll kill me. Or turn into a dragon. Or fry eggs off the cement patio. Those are things a dream dad would do.

But this father, my father, he stands up, walks to me, and hugs me. I can feel the force of him even if I can't quite feel him.

Mom continues to scream.

I can't move. My eyes are closed against his shoulder. I wish I could close my ears against Mom's screams.

And then, as if Dad heard my thoughts, there's a crack, and the screaming stops.

I open my eyes. Mom's cheek is blooming like a rose. Her variety was red, too. It was called Morning Glory. Because her name is Gloria, and she says every sunrise is a miracle.

"You hit Mom!" the blue-haired girl exclaims.

"I'm sorry, Melissa, but your mother's in shock. Gloria, you're in shock," Dad says. "Snap out of it. It's her."

"It can't be," Mom says.

"It is," Dad says. "I'd know her anywhere."

"How?" Mom asks. "How can it be her?"

Dad holds me at arm's length, grazing my face with his thumb. The gesture is so loving, it's hard to reconcile it coming

24

from the same hand that just slapped Mom. But it *is* his hand. I see the scar on his finger from when it got crushed by a loose cement mixer.

"Miracle," he says.

BRIAN
Twenty-Nine Years Before

The day Brian Crane met his wife did not start out well. He'd forgotten to set his alarm clock, or it had failed to go off. It didn't matter because by the time his roommate shook him awake, he had twenty minutes to get to campus before his organic chemistry midterm. The exam was worth 30 percent of the grade. He had to maintain a 3.6 GPA to keep his scholarship.

He did not shower, did not eat, did not pass go. It was raining and normally he would take the bus to campus, but he had no time, so he asked his roommate if he could borrow his bike.

He got to campus drenched, shivering, and with two minutes to spare before the test started. He threw the chain around the bike and ran inside the chemistry building. The TAs were passing out the exams just as he sat down. One gave him a look: *Cutting it close, Mister.*

He had trouble focusing, unable to shake the feeling that

he'd forgotten something, like maybe he'd left the stove on, except he didn't cook (what college sophomore did?). He yanked his attention back to the work—heterocyclic compounds, polymers, he knew this stuff—but as soon as he scribbled an answer, that sense of unfinished business gnawed at him again. It was probably retroactive, worrying after the fact that he'd forgotten to set the alarm. He reminded himself it had all ended well. He'd made it on time and he was prepared for the test, but the feeling did not go away.

O chem was one of his strongest subjects, but he took the entire testing period to complete the exam, with not a minute left over to check his answers. When the proctors called time, he handed in his test and shuffled outside, where the rain had lessened to a drizzle and the sky was a bright, blaring gray. He squinted, his head aching because he had skipped coffee and breakfast in the morning's rush. He turned left, walking toward the student union, urgently needing some food and caffeine, but as he approached the building, that nagging feeling of having forgotten something grew more intense. He decided to go home, to check the stove and the front door, double-check his alarm clock for tomorrow.

As he scanned the racks, trying to recall what his roommate's bicycle looked like, his gaze snagged on a young woman, pacing back and forth. She was beautiful, in spite of the look on her face, which was lethal.

When she saw him approach the bikes, her eyes narrowed and he realized the lethalness was aimed at him. It should have scared him. But it didn't.

"Is this yours?" she asked, pointing at the silver Mongoose.

It wasn't. It was his roommate's. But even if it had been a total stranger's bike, Brian would have claimed it. He nodded and she held up the chain, which in his haste, he now saw, he had locked not just to his roommate's bike but also to the one next to it, a purple Schwinn with a basket.

"Can you unlock it, please?" She glanced at the silver watch around her slender wrist. Her skin was fair, almost pink, dusted with freckles.

"I'm so, so sorry," Brian said. As he unlocked the chain, he hastily told her the story of his morning, apologizing every fifth word, because he was truly sorry, and also because he didn't want to let this girl go just yet. "Let me make it up to you," he added. "Take you to breakfast. Or lunch. Or dinner."

"I can't. I'm almost late for my exam, which is on the other side of campus," she said.

"After your exam, then."

"That's in two hours."

"I'll wait."

"I have to work at three."

"Where do you work?"

"Our Lady of Salvation."

Brian vaguely knew that this was a Catholic church, a place that was only memorable to him because its bells had rusted through and never rang, which Brian thought was an apt metaphor for religion.

Brian was a scientist. He hoped to become a biochemical

researcher or an industrial engineer. He did not believe in God. Want to see a miracle? Look at the neon glory of mitochondria under an electric microscope. Of hydrated ferric acid turning a church bell from bright orange copper to algae green. If this girl was some sort of Bible thumper, then she was not for him.

But as he watched her ride away, that feeling of having forgotten something returned like a fire engine screaming in his head. This girl, who he'd never met, but whose bike he'd accidentally chained his borrowed one to, was the fire.

He jumped on his roommate's bike and pedaled fast and hard to the other side of the campus, catching up with her just as she was dismounting by the history building.

"I'm sorry," he said, breathless. "I'm not stalking you, but if it's okay, I'd like to wait for you."

She looked at him for what felt like a long time. It was absurd what he was asking, ridiculous to expect her to say anything beyond "Buzz off!"

She locked her bike. "Suit yourself," she said, and walked into the building to sit for her exam.

Brian was still hungry, and he knew, logically, he had plenty of time to grab a burrito and a coffee and be back before she finished; even if she was a fast test taker, she couldn't be that fast. But he was not about to risk it. So he sat on a bench near the bike racks and waited in the drizzle.

When she emerged from the test, the sun had come out. She stood still for a moment, head up, basking in the rays. He thought he'd never seen anything more beautiful, until seconds later, she put her hand to her forehead and scanned the area, looking for him.

He stood up from his bench and waved at her. She waved back. That nagging feeling of missing something vanished into the sun-dappled air.

AMBER

As soon as the sun goes down, I feign a yawn and say I'm tired. I'm not. Not even a little, but I desperately want to fall asleep and wake up to find this is all a wild dream. But as the hours creep by, sleep refuses to come. I do all my tricks, focusing on my breathing, reciting a Shakespeare sonnet over and over, but nothing works. I don't drift off, even for a second.

When I got sick as a kid, Mom would be the one to come into my room throughout the night, putting a hand on my forehead to make sure I was okay, but she disappeared into her bedroom not long after Dad arrived and has not come out. So it falls to Dad, then, who comes into my room over and over again. I pretend to sleep. I love my dad, but I want to wake up and have him just be regular Dad and me be regular Amber.

I think of the prayer Mom taught us to recite before bed when we were kids: *Now I lay me down to sleep. I pray the Lord my soul to keep. If I should die before I wake, I pray the Lord my soul to take.*

If I died, why didn't anyone take my soul?

If I died, why I am here?

One time in catechism, Liam Heller asked Father Mercer if hell was really pitchforks and devils. "Worse," Father Mercer replied. "Think of your scariest nightmare. Come true. Forever. That's hell."

Could I have landed in hell? I know I did not-great things. I lied. I gossiped. I was not always nice to other people, but I thought I had time to remedy that, to confess and become a better person.

What were the seven deadly sins? I go down the list: pride, greed, wrath, lust.

Lust.

Am I in hell because I had premarital sex?

"Calvin!" I cry, jolting up in bed.

"Will you wait for me?" Calvin asked when he was considering joining the army to pay for college.

"I'll wait for you forever," I told him.

I shiver from the cold even though I have the duvet and two extra blankets. Light peeks through the tiny holes in the blackout shades, evidence of Mr. Fluff's claw art. I pat my bed the way that used to summon him from his hiding place in my closet. I need him to climb on my chest and purr, sending that warm feeling through me.

"Mr. Fluff?" I whisper, tapping the bed again, but nothing

happens. I do the math. Seven years. The cat was already old. When Dad comes in again, I don't bother pretending to sleep. "When did Mr. Fluff die?" I ask him.

He flips on the bedroom light. "About four or five years ago." He walks toward me, his hair a staticky mess, the gold of his hazel eyes shot through with red. "Did you sleep well?"

"Like a log," I lie. "Did you?"

"Not a wink," he says. "I watched you almost all night. Just like when you were a baby. I kept thinking if I fell asleep I'd wake up and you'd be gone."

I don't tell Dad I had the same idea, only mine was a hope that I'd wake to find all this a dream. "I'm here," I say weakly, shivering again.

"Are you cold?" Dad asks.

"A little," I admit. I don't want to tell him how truly cold I am. What if he wants to do something like take my temperature? What if it comes out not 98.6 but 88.2 or 64.7 or so cold the thermometer won't even register?

"Let's get some breakfast in you," he says.

"Okay."

I follow Dad into the living room. It's dim, the shades are drawn, and there are blankets and a pillow on the couch. I guess he didn't want to keep Mom up last night with his vigil.

Missy springs up from the table when she sees me and gathers me in a hug. I can feel the pressure of it, but not the heat of her body. "I can't believe you're here," she says. "Really here. I'm so happy."

"Where's Mom?"

"She's still in her room," Dad says. "She's having a hard time processing this." He goes to the pantry and starts rooting around. "Your death hit her really hard."

"Yeah, I can tell by how happy she was to see me again."

"She doesn't believe it's you," Missy says.

"I get it. But hello, who else am I?"

"Miracles can be hard to accept," Dad replies. "People didn't believe it when Jesus brought Lazarus back from the dead."

"*You're* quoting scripture?" I ask. "Aren't you supposed to be an atheist?"

"I was. Until yesterday." Dad turns back to the pantry. "What are you craving? Pancakes. Chocolate cake. Coffee. Do you drink coffee?"

I never drank coffee. It felt like such a trick to me how the aroma was so delicious and the taste so bitter. There's a pot on, but when I breathe in, I can't even smell it.

"Can we turn up the heat?"

"I can do better than that. I'll build you a nice fire." Dad turns to Missy. "Do we still have firewood?"

"Out back, under the tarp."

Dad looks at me, smiling. "I'll build you a blaze. Get you nice and warm."

While Dad goes rooting through the yard, Missy goes to the hall closet, pulling down one of the boxes I'd mistaken for college gear. "I thought you might want to see some of the other things that were written about you after you died. If that's not too morbid."

"Depends. Did people say nice things?"

"Super nice," she says.

"Then I definitely want to see."

"I figured. It's like the dream, isn't it? Getting to hear people eulogize you."

"Maybe that was *your* dream, but you were always weird."

It's not the first time I've called my sister that, and before, she'd get all shrivel-faced and upset, but now she just laughs as she rips the tape off one of the boxes and lifts the flaps. "It smells like you."

"Really? I have a smell?"

"Everyone has a smell," she says. "Mom smells like lavender. Dad smells like cement and spearmint. And you smell like, well, like you." She inhales the box. "You probably can't smell it because it's you."

Maybe. Or maybe I can't smell it because I can't smell. I take another breath. I know our house smelled like something. When I would come home from camp after the summer, it always hit me. But now? I get nothing.

I peer inside the box. It's a hodgepodge of school things: a poem I won a prize for in fourth grade, a play I wrote sophomore year, the clay handprints I made in kindergarten, and other random homework assignments. I can't believe they saved all this. But maybe what's clutter when you're alive becomes treasure when you're not.

Missy pulls down another box. It's full of my personal keepsakes: the scrapbook Casey and Alexa made for my sweet sixteen. A calligraphy print of *Amber*, transliterated into Chinese, from

Aunt Pauline. A program from *Sweet Charity* when I played Nickie Pignatelli. The envelope where I put the dried corsage Calvin got me for junior prom. High school yearbooks, including the one from senior year, which I haven't seen before. Yearbooks are handed out the last week of school. Seniors get theirs a few days before everyone else, and it's a ritual to spend the last two days of school rehearsing for graduation and then loafing in the quad, signing one another's books. There's always lots of hugging and crying. If you aren't a senior, you watch the spectacle with envy (no classes, all that drama) and anticipation (one day it will be your turn).

I expect my yearbook to be blank, because I wasn't there for graduation, but when I flip through the pages, there are more messages than in any of my previous yearbooks. It's not like I was unpopular. I had lots of friends, but I'd never infiltrated the top tier with girls like Odessa Lumley, who drew a giant broken heart in my yearbook and wrote: *Miss you so much each and every day.*

"It was too late to put your memorial in this yearbook," Missy says. "So they added it to next year's. Want to see?"

Missy reaches for another yearbook, the one that came out during what should have been my first year of college. Opposite the back cover is a full-page spread of a mural, with rainbows and clouds and angels. There's a quote but it's too small to make out.

"It's from Virginia Woolf," Missy says.

"Ugh. We read *To the Lighthouse* in English lit. I hated it."

36

"I liked it," Missy says.

"Of course you did. What did the quote say?"

"'Someone has to die in order that the rest of us should value life more.'"

"Morbid much?" I joke.

"There was debate about it being cruel or whatever, but Mr. King—remember him?—said it meant that often we don't appreciate our own lives until someone else loses theirs and to honor you we should live to the fullest."

"Glad to be of service." I peer at the photo. "Where is this?"

"In the breezeway, near the black box theater," Missy says. "My locker's right there so I see you every day."

"God. You go to Kennedy. How weird is that?"

"Compared to what?" Missy deadpans.

"Ha." I pause to look at my sister. "You're funny. When did you become funny?"

"I always was funny. You just never noticed because you had a stick up your butt."

I pause to look at my backside. "It appears to have disappeared with my death."

"Ha!" Missy says. "You're funny now, too."

I flip through the senior yearbook, looking for a message, or more like a drawing, from Calvin, but I don't see one. I scan for pictures of us—there were tons in junior year—but I only see a group shot of him, me, Alexa, and Casey.

I riffle through the box. "Where's my sophomore yearbook?"

"Here," Missy replies, handing me another one.

"That's freshman year. Where's my sophomore year?"

"They all should be in here," Missy says.

"It's not." I start to fling things out of the box. "Where is it?"

"Calm down. It's right here," Missy says, handing it to me.

I need to see it. Calvin. I flip to the page where it should be. The page that goes from *H* through *M*, near his picture. That's where he'd drawn it. That's where he'd started it.

CALVIN
Nine Years Before

Calvin privately griped that he wasn't the thick lughead people assumed, but maybe he *was* stupid. It had been profoundly dumb to confess to Dean what he'd written in Amber's yearbook on the last day of school. Dean had laughed so hard he'd sent an arc of Pabst Blue Ribbon onto Calvin. "Didn't know you had a pussy, Calvin," Dean said. And then he said, "Meow."

Meow. Calvin had been hearing it all summer long. He and Dean both worked for the same landscaping company and any time Calvin got something cushy, like mowing the Flannagan lawn with the tractor, as opposed to the more backbreaking job of building the retaining wall for the Wilsons, Dean would whisper in his ear, "Good thing you got the easy gig," and then he would meow. When Dean found out that Calvin had refused one of the female clients who'd started to be, um, attentive, asking Calvin in for lemonade, to rub some zinc oxide onto his sunburnt nose, he didn't stop meowing for the better part of a week.

Yeah, Dean was an asshole. But at the same time, he was a good friend, dragging Calvin to all the parties he was invited to that summer, and some that he wasn't, in search of Amber. Every time Calvin would show up at some pool party or kegger, he'd look for Amber, but she was never there. So he'd go home and draw her—this he didn't tell Dean; he wasn't *that* stupid—as he'd done all year long in ELA, where he'd sat behind her, staring at the back of her neck, barely listening to Mr. King go on about sentence structure or similes because he was too busy making doodles: Amber using a pencil to put her hair up in a bun. Or Amber's freckles that showered her shoulders. Or Amber's bracelet that slid up her wrist when she raised her hand to answer a question. If he could draw how she sounded, the uplilt in her voice when she wasn't sure of an answer, or how she smelled, like sunshine and lemons, he would have.

He got so used to drawing her that it became second nature. So when on the last day of school, she handed him her yearbook to sign, before he could think about what he was doing, he'd drawn a picture of her, right in the margin of the page near his own picture, so it looked like his portrait was looking at her. If that weren't bad enough, he'd drawn thought bubbles leading to a heart and a question mark.

Meow.

When he saw what he'd done, he started to scratch it out, to transform it into something less damning. But then someone asked Amber for her yearbook to sign and she grabbed it from him and handed it off before he'd had a chance to fix it. The one thing in his favor was that she hadn't seen it then. Maybe she'd never see it. Or maybe by the time fall came back around, she would forget. He would forget it. It would all be forgotten.

Except he'd gotten drunk over the Fourth of July and confessed to Dean not just the idiotic thing he'd drawn in Amber's yearbook, but worse, that he was obsessing over this girl, prompting Dean to ride his ass but also to drag him to all the parties, like this one, Lee Franklin's Labor Day blast. He had no hope of seeing her at the party, or at school when it started next week. Amber was smart, on the AP track, unlike Calvin, who'd had to repeat second grade because he couldn't read right. They wouldn't be in any of the same classes. A devastating relief.

Partiers spilled out of the house. Lee was a senior, popular because he played varsity basketball and because his parents had a weekend house and left him home alone to throw blowouts like this one. Everyone seemed to be here.

Calvin didn't want to be. He liked kicking back with some beers and some bros but he didn't like parties. It was his size again. Being so tall and broad—six foot and two hundred fifty pounds; a refrigerator, Coach called him—made it next to impossible to blend in. As he climbed the porch steps and walked into the party, he felt like Godzilla pushing through the throngs of normal-sized bodies. And anyhow, Amber hadn't been at any of the other parties, so why would she be at this one? He pulled out his phone to text Dean to say he wasn't staying but someone jostled him, sending his phone flying out of his hands and under the couch.

He crouched down on his hands and knees, reaching for his phone, but it was too far back and he couldn't grab it. He pulled back up and smacked into the coffee table, sending a row of Solo cups skittering. All the frustration of his size, of his stupidity, his meowness, welled up inside him making him want to punch something.

"Looking for this?"

He wasn't facing her, but that voice, he'd know it anywhere. He had listened to it recite poems and stories and plays all year. He had imagined that voice saying his name. Saying she loved him.

Meow.

He lumbered up and there she was, Amber Crane, level to his chest and holding his phone before her like an offering. The wave of frustration crescendoed into a whole different feeling. Instead of wanting to punch someone, he wanted to kiss someone. More specifically, he wanted to kiss her. And in that moment, unlikely as it seemed, he felt like maybe, one day, he would.

"Yes," he said, taking the phone and looking at her. "I am."

AMBER

When the fire is built, Missy packs up the boxes but I hang on to the sophomore yearbook, my finger tabbed to the page with Calvin's portrait and the sketch he drew of me.

"I made a real inferno for you, Amber," Dad says, nudging the logs with the poker.

And he did. Five logs are blazing but they don't warm me at all. One pops, sending a flurry of sparks, a few landing on my bare arm, but I feel nothing, and there's no mark. Still, I rub it like there is, so Dad and Missy don't think that I came back different, or defective, and start screaming like Mom.

We all sit there in silence, no one sure of what to say. To be fair, even if I hadn't died, this kind of forced togetherness would've felt awkward.

"So?" I ask after an interminable five minutes. "Now what?"

"Now *this*," Dad says. "I could sit here with you for seven years to make up for the lost time."

"I think it would get boring after a year, or even an hour." I turn to my sister. "And don't you have school?"

"I'm taking a day off from school and work, so I'm free. What do you want to do?"

I rub the top of the yearbook. I didn't even see Calvin's cute sketch until the night before I left to be a counselor at camp for the summer, when it was too late to do anything about it. I missed him all summer, even though I hardly knew him. Suddenly, I miss him now.

"I want to see Calvin."

Dad and Missy exchange a look.

"I don't think that's a good idea," Dad says.

"Why? Because of the age difference?" Calvin would be twenty-five now. But supposedly I'm twenty-four, and besides, how can that matter?

"For lots of reasons," Dad says, shooting Missy another look.

"What reasons?"

No one answers.

"Ohmygod, did he die, too?"

I like to think that if he had, I would've known. That he'd have found me. When Gammy died, Mom didn't cry. She said she'd see her again in heaven. She believed it. And so I believed it. But I didn't see Gammy, either. Or if I did, I don't remember. Or maybe I never went to heaven. I'm still not positive I'm not in hell now.

The fire crackles.

"No," Missy says. "He's still alive. He's just different."

44

"Melissa," Dad admonishes.

"Does he live here?"

"Yes," Missy says, and when Dad starts to interrupt her, she cuts him off. "Sorry, Dad, it's her right to know," she says before turning back to me. "He works at the Bitter End."

"That dive bar downtown?" I'm trying to understand why Calvin is working there. "Did he finish business school? Is he, like, managing it?"

No one says anything and now I'm starting to get pissed. I know my parents think Calvin and I are—or were—too young to be so serious, but we had a plan. We'd go to the same college, get married after graduation, like my parents did. Then he'd support me while I got my teaching degree and I'd support us when he was in business school, and after that we'd be rich. Their disapproval was so hypocritical. Mom and Dad met in college. We met in high school. What difference do a few years make if you love someone and they love you? And now it's been seven years. Enough time wasted.

"I want to see him!"

"I don't think that's wise," Dad says.

"Well, if I've really been dead seven years, then I'm twenty-four now and I'm legally an adult and can do what I want."

"I believe we have exited the realm of legal technicalities," Dad says. "And you shouldn't see him."

"Why, is he married?" It seems inconceivable that he could be with anyone else, but then again a lot's seeming inconceivable right now.

"Not that I know of," Missy says.

I exhale. "Then what is it?"

Another log explodes, sending sparks up the mantel, which was where Mom and Dad's wedding portrait always hung. I loved that picture, not because it was such a great photo; it's not. Mom looks tired and Dad's tie is crooked. But they were so young, at the beginning of everything, and they stayed in love. You could see it in the ways they touched each other's arms as they were doing something so normal, like passing the parmesan cheese. This was what I wanted with Calvin. It made no sense that they didn't approve of him.

But the portrait isn't there. And the pile of bedding is still on the couch. Mom and Dad hated sleeping apart. Even when Dad had pneumonia and was up hacking at night for weeks or when Mom was up until two a.m. studying for her boards, they refused to sleep separately. And now they are.

Dad puts the poker back and brushes the ash off his hands. That's when I notice he's not wearing his wedding band. I've never once seen either him or Mom without their rings. Missy and I used to try to get them to take them off so we could read the secret inscription inside but they said that was between them. "And the jeweler," Mom would say, and they'd trade one of their conspiratorial smiles.

I think of how Mom looked, haggard and old and changed in a way that I only now fully appreciate. It's not just the gray hairs and wrinkles that make her face look like a napkin ironed wrong. When she was with my father, it was always like there was a light glowing behind her eyes, bright when he was around, dimmer when he had to go to some convention or work late. Yesterday, the light was out.

And now I see it. Mom and Dad. They're not together anymore.

GLORIA
Twenty-Six Years Before

When Gloria first saw the wedding bands, she cried. They were so plain, so ugly, so small. She'd been raised on a steady diet of princess stories, had attended her fair share of wedding masses. She'd been imagining her own nuptials since her first communion.

This wedding was going to be nothing like the one she'd conjured up. Everything was going to be cheap, done on the fly. She knew what people were thinking: shotgun. But it wasn't birth she was racing against; it was death.

Her father had been diagnosed with stage-four kidney cancer six weeks earlier. In all Gloria's wedding fantasies, her father walked her down the aisle. When she told Brian about the diagnosis, he said they should get married as soon as possible.

Gloria had known she would marry Brian since that very first day. She'd been eating the burrito he'd brought for her on her work break when she'd looked up and just had a feeling that he was her future. If that sounded ludicrous, well, Brian claimed to have known even sooner than that, from the minute he'd accidentally chained his bike to hers. So it wasn't like getting married now was a major pivot. But they'd had a plan mapped out. They both were applying to graduate school, him for biochemical engineering, her for speech pathology. After they finished, they'd get married, then buy a house together and start a family. "Getting married now is not our plan," she reminded Brian.

"Life is what happens when you're busy making other plans," Brian replied.

"I hope you're not pregnant!" Gloria's mother said when she announced the rushed nuptials.

"I hope you are!" said Gloria's little sister, Pauline. "I wanna be an auntie!"

"I'm not pregnant," Gloria said, her face coloring, because even though they'd been careful, theoretically she could be. They were having premarital sex, with protection, both things her mother strongly disapproved of. Probably marital sex, too, which would explain why her parents had only had two children, a decade apart.

"I can't help you plan your wedding; I've got too much to deal with now with your father," her mother said. "Also, I'm afraid we can't spare any money right now."

"I'll help you plan the wedding," Pauline said. "And I have twenty-three dollars from the magazine sale. You can have that!"

"Thanks, P," she said, hugging her sister, wondering how someone so open and loving could come from a woman as cold and closed as their mother. Even Gloria wasn't naturally warm, and whatever warmth she did possess had come first from Pauline and later from Brian.

When she told Brian there was no money for the kind of wedding she'd envisioned, he said it didn't matter. "We have our whole lives to be married. To throw parties and wear fancy clothes and buy jewelry. Your father walking you down the aisle is what matters."

Gloria knew this was true. So she'd bought a dress, secondhand. She'd booked the church hall for a Thursday night, when the price was reduced. She'd chosen the cheapest catering package and hired a student to deejay. She'd forbidden Brian to buy her an engagement ring. Better to save for a down payment. Once they were married, they needed a house and neither wanted to waste money on rent. Graduate school would have to wait for both of them.

But the wedding rings. They were so plain. Thin and silver, which would tarnish.

"We'll polish them," Brian said. "I'm sure we'll get a little tarnished, too."

But when she went to the jeweler to pick up the rings, she cried. It was not about the rings. Or just the rings. There was her father, so ill. She was losing him just as she was gaining Brian. It made her feel like one had caused the other. "Aren't you always saying that God never gives you more than you can bear?" Brian asked her. "Maybe God chose this exact moment to take your father because he knew you could bear it with me. We could bear it together."

"You don't believe in God," she had said through her tears.

This had always stood between them, her faith, his lack of it. He'd asked her if she minded that he didn't believe in God— once, after they started dating and again before he proposed—and both times she'd answered honestly. Yes, she wished he shared her faith. But she also knew that she was meant to meet him. His locking that bike to hers was no accident; it was a miracle from God that she would not squander.

"I have enough faith for the both of us," she told him each time. And she believed this. But that didn't mean she didn't want nicer rings.

"What's the matter?" the jeweler asked, offering Gloria a handkerchief for her tears.

Gloria told him about her father's illness, the bare-bones wedding, what Brian had said about getting a husband, losing a father. The circle of life. "Nothing is like I thought it would be, and this ring doesn't feel special."

The jeweler was sympathetic. "I'm sorry about your father. As for the ring, it's not the metal or diamond or setting that makes it special. It's the person wearing it," he said, before lowering his voice. "Don't tell anyone my secret or I'll go out of business."

Gloria dabbed her cheeks, laughed a bit.

"I like your husband's take. It's the circle of life, on your finger."

"But must it be such a plain circle of life?" Gloria asked.

"What some people do," the jeweler replied, "is inscribe something on the ring, something meaningful and personal." He smiled, adding, "It's no extra charge."

A week later, her father walked Gloria down the aisle. She and Brian exchanged the rings, unadorned save for what she'd asked the jeweler to engrave on them.

Four weeks after that, Gloria buried her father.

Later on, after they'd bought a house and Brian had started his business and they had, if not a lot of money, enough for the diamond ring she'd never gotten, Brian suggested an upgrade. But by then she'd grown to love the rings, round and plain and reminiscent of the links in the metal chain that had bound Brian's borrowed bike to hers, Brian to her. The thought of taking off the band was unbearable. She told Brian she was happy with what they had.

AMBER

Me being dead and then alive doesn't feel as wrong as Mom and Dad being apart. They were meant to be together forever. Like me and Calvin were.

I need to see Calvin. To believe that love can survive.

I go back to my room, claiming to need a nap. I wait until Dad's truck pulls out before I poke my head into the hallway. Mom and Dad's—no, Mom's—door is still closed, the Do Not Disturb sign I made her when she started graduate school hanging on the door. Missy is in her room, on her computer. I creep past and slip into the garage, wheeling my bike out before jumping on and pedaling as fast as I can toward downtown.

I try to picture the last time I saw Calvin. Yesterday, on my way home, it seemed like I'd just seen him, but when I try to pinpoint a specific memory, it's fuzzy, like trying to read a book in a dream.

Here's what I do remember: Calvin and I getting our college acceptances to the same school, feeling like this was the first step in our life together. Calvin and I having sex for the first time after junior prom. Calvin and I exchanging our first kiss at the bake sale. All those firsts. But even the memories feel distant now, like memories of memories, the way Mom and Dad's stories of when they first met do. I wasn't there, obviously, but I've heard the tales of their meeting, of the wedding, of Mom crying at the jeweler's, so often that they have become mine.

I've never been to the Bitter End, but I know where it is. Everyone does. It's been around forever, a low windowless building with a blinking neon sign on a corner next to a parking lot. The town declared the sign a landmark so it's not allowed to be taken down, no matter who owns the place. It's changed hands a bunch of times, but it's always been a dump. It's like the name has cursed it.

When I push open the door, a tiny bell tinkles, such a sweet sound for such a dark, dank place. It's nearly empty, with only one couple arguing at a corner table. Which sums up the vibe.

How could Calvin—who worked so hard to avoid this kind of thing—have wound up here?

The only other person around is the bartender. He's older, maybe around Aunt Pauline's age, and is wearing a bandanna low across his forehead. I approach him to ask if I could speak to the manager, because Calvin must be in charge. His gaze is downward as he writes in some sort of ledger and doesn't look up when I approach.

I clear my throat. "Excuse me," I say.

His head whips up and that's when I see the face, so familiar and not at the same time, and then the ledger, which isn't a ledger. It's a sketchbook, full of doodles and drawings I would know anywhere.

"Calvin?"

How can this be Calvin? Who was big, substantial, like a monster truck, he used to joke self-deprecatingly. He was self-conscious about his size, but I loved it because you would never guess that kind of body could house that kind of heart. His heft made him feel solid. Made me feel safe.

But this person is so thin—it's like one gust of wind and he'd be knocked right over. He's gaping at me like I'm a stranger.

"Calvin, it's me. Amber."

He blinks and says nothing.

"I'm Amber. Your Amber."

A strangled sound escapes from his mouth as he pushes himself away from the bar and for a horrible second, I think he's going to do what my mom did: scream, hide, reject me. But he catapults his entire body over the bar and grabs me by the shoulders. His eyes blaze with something as he raises his hand and for one brief moment I think he's going to hit me.

But he doesn't. He pulls my head into his chest and I let out a sigh of relief from the deepest part of me. Calvin. My forever love. Here.

I pull him toward me, reaching up to take off the bandanna. To see Calvin. My Calvin. Calvin's lips. Calvin's hands. Calvin's stubble. Calvin's spit. I want to drink it all in.

He reaches behind me to lift me up. His girth may be diminished but he is still tall, and he lifts me easily. I swing my legs around his hips, hanging on for dear life.

Walking backward, he pushes us through double swinging saloon doors, and then opens another door, closing it behind him with a powerful kick. He lays me down on a couch. He climbs on top of me and I wait for it, for the weight of him. The permanence. The safety. But even with his body on mine, I don't feel anything. It's like he's hovering.

My shoes come off. My pants. My shirt. My bra.

I start to shiver. It's freezing in here, even colder than it was at home.

Calvin stands up to kick off his shoes, his jeans. I see his desire. I used to have so much for him. But it's like something on a distant shore. Is this a byproduct of coming back to life? Does it take a bit of time for the systems to fire back up?

I grab at his shirt. I want it off. I need to feel all of him, to bring me back, truly back. I yank again, tugging so hard at the shirt it rips down the center, the shirt hanging open like a gash. Underneath, Calvin's once powerful chest is as concave as a collapsed cake.

I gasp. "Calvin!"

He blinks once, then twice, and looks right at me. They're his eyes, and they're not his eyes. They look empty, like a home once lived in but now abandoned. *What happened to him?* I think.

"Amber," he says. It sounds less like he's saying my name

than answering my unspoken question.

What happened to him? I happened to him.

His expression has changed, a dark curtain blocking out the dim light.

"You're not Amber," he says.

"I am," I say. "I know it seems impossible, but I am."

Calvin flattens his palms against his eyes and pushes hard, the sinews in his diminished muscles straining. I'm scared he might pop out his eyes or something. He is so strong. Or was.

"You're not Amber." His voice is ragged and desperate. "Amber died."

"I know I did. But I'm back now. I know it makes no sense, but I'm here. And I still love you. I *forever* love you."

The room goes still. Calvin leans over and heaves into a bucket, only unlike when I puked, something comes out, and though I can't smell it, I can tell it has the same boozy reek of defeat that emanates throughout the bar.

"Calvin," I cry again, but he's already yanking up his pants and running out of the room. I put on my clothes and chase after him, but when I get back to the bar, it's empty now, save for the echo of the bell ringing over the door.

CASEY

Eight Years Before

Casey Locke did not understand why people made such a big deal over weddings. You got to dress up, sure, but never as nice as the bride or bridesmaids, who had their hair and makeup done professionally. Then you had to sit there with a straight face as people made all sorts of bogus promises about loving each other forever.

Casey might have been only sixteen years old, but she knew this was a crock. Marriage was a cage, maybe a diamond-encrusted one, but still a cage. Just look at her parents.

They'd made her come to this wedding, even though she barely knew the couple. The groom was some colleague of her dad's. She'd tried to get out of it until her dad had pleaded, "Please, princess. I want to show off our beautiful family." Plus, to sweeten the deal, he said she could get a new dress.

And so now, here they were, the beautiful Locke family,

milling during the cocktail hour before the reception. Her parents held hands and smiled with too much teeth as they were greeted by her father's employees, some of whom remarked on just what a woman Casey was becoming, eyeing the low-cut sleeveless silk sheath she'd bought for the wedding with an expression that suggested this was not necessarily a compliment. As soon as they moved on, Casey's mom's smile dropped and she complained about the open bar serving only wine and beer, which she called "cheap," or the bride's beaded dress, which she deemed "tacky."

Speaking of cheap and tacky, in the corner of the room, a woman in a blue-spangled dress started playing the piano. It was the song "Memories" from *Cats*.

"Hey, Dad," Casey said in between all the glad-handing. "I'm thinking of trying out for the school musical."

It had been Amber's idea. "We'll have so much fun," she'd said in that annoyingly gushy way of hers. "They're doing *Guys and Dolls*. You could be Adelaide and I'll be Sarah."

"Why, because Sarah's so pure and Adelaide's a slut?" Casey had replied, half joking, half not. She knew she had a reputation at school as someone who "got around." The irony was, she hadn't even had sex while Amber, the pure one, had. But she let people believe the rumors. It gave her an edge. Her father said it was important to have an edge.

"What? No!" Amber had replied, aghast. "Sarah's more of a soprano part, that's all." It hadn't been an insult, exactly. But it felt like one. Amber was a really good singer, all those years of practicing in her church choir and going to her theater camp.

"I've got better things to do than hang out with a bunch of drama geeks," Casey had replied. But later, after she'd thought about it, she'd reconsidered. At least she'd have some alone time with Amber. Calvin was practically glued to her side these days but he wouldn't be at play rehearsal.

"Can you even sing?" her father asked now, though it didn't sound like a question so much as an accusation. *You can't sing*.

Casey hadn't been in church choir since she was eight, but she could hold a tune. Maybe there was a voice even better than Amber's lurking inside her. And if there wasn't, the PTA was always scrounging for money to pay for drama productions, and if her dad wrote a large check, that would give her an edge.

"That piano player's really good," her father said. Casey watched as he walked over to her, pulling a bill out of his wallet. Instead of dropping it in the tip bowl on top of the piano, he handed it to her. She smiled and put the bill into her bra. It was a fifty. The piano player definitely wasn't that good.

Soon they were invited into the reception, held in the same room the ceremony had taken place in, only now a temporary dance floor had been laid over the area where the bride and groom had declared their forever love.

Casey sat down at their assigned table. The chairs had tall backs covered in white taffeta, like they were brides. She kicked the shoe off her left foot, where a blister was forming on her heel. She pushed the shoe against the chair leg, the pain strangely satisfying.

The salad plates were already on the table and a server in

60

a tuxedo began to distribute bread rolls like a pitcher lobbing fastballs, dropping one onto her mother's plate before she could refuse it on account of her self-diagnosed gluten allergy, which Casey knew to be a calorie allergy. Her father ate both rolls and then stood up. "I'm going to go to the little boys' room before the rubber chicken arrives."

Several minutes passed, long enough for a second server to deliver the entrées. Casey watched her mother mentally calculate the calories in the chicken breast, the brown gravy, the mashed potatoes, the broccoli. Casey knew she would eat maybe half the chicken, sauce scraped off, a bite of the potatoes, and all the greens.

And sure enough, her mother began to painstakingly knife the gravy off the chicken. While she was distracted with her surgical work, Casey shoved her foot back in the shoe and stood up. "I'll be right back," she said, heading toward the bar, which she hoped would be unattended. Maybe she could chug back a few unfinished drinks. On an empty stomach, it would work fast and if she didn't eat much, the buzz might last for most of this horrible reception.

The bar was mostly empty. Just one guy wolfing down a plate of the crab puffs and spring rolls that had been passed during the cocktail hour. He looked a little familiar: dark hair, Asian, tattoos, the guy version of a resting bitch face. He was too busy eating to pay her any attention, so she sidled up to one of the tall tables in the far corner where several discarded glasses of wine remained. Half full. And who said Casey was not an optimist!

She downed two and was just about to snatch a third when

she heard a girlish giggle. In the far corner, the piano player was sitting at a table. And the person making her laugh was Casey's father.

It was a not-so-well-kept secret in their family that Casey's father had what her mother called "a tendency to roam." Which meant, Casey understood, he had affairs. "But he always comes back to me," her mother said, once, through tears, a sunk bottle of Chardonnay on the table. Casey was not sure she'd ever witnessed anything more pathetic. She vowed then and there never, ever, to wind up as powerless as her insipid mother.

The guy at the bar was standing now, holding a camera—that was why he was familiar; he was the wedding photographer—watching her looking at her dad. He wore an expression of pity, which pissed Casey off far more than her dad flirting with some cheap slut did. "Asshole," she hissed at him as she made her way back to the dining room.

Her dad returned a few minutes later, smiling at her. Casey felt a curtain of despair descend. Why did her dad make her come to the wedding, when he couldn't be bothered to pay any attention to her?

She watched her mother cut her chicken into centimeter-sized cubes. At the head table, the groom whispered something to the bride that made her laugh, revealing the lipstick on her front teeth. Casey thought of the way the piano player had tucked her father's fifty next to her breasts. Nope. She was not going to audition for the musical, she decided. There was no way she was playing second fiddle to Amber. Casey deserved to have something all her own.

AMBER

Dad's truck is still gone when I get home so I think I've managed to avoid trouble. But when I go inside, Mom is sitting at the kitchen table, phone in hand. She slams it down and rushes at me, and for a second I think she's going to hug me, but she just shakes me.

"Stop," I cry. "You're hurting me." She isn't, not in my body anyway. But the flatness in her eyes, the blankness in Calvin's— people who love you don't look at you like that.

"Where were you?" she demands.

"I—I found out about you and Dad," I say. "I was upset!"

"Where did you go?"

"I just rode my bike around." This is only half a lie. I did ride my bike.

"Did anyone see you?"

"No." This, too, feels like only half a lie because I'm not sure Calvin *did* see me.

Mom's face is a mask of fury. "Do you have any idea what kind of trouble you could cause?"

"No, Mom, I don't. They never taught back-from-the-dead protocol in Sunday school."

Mom touches a hand to her cheek like I've slapped her. "Go to your room!"

"You can't send me to my room. I'm twenty-four now." I look at my reflection in the oven door. I don't look twenty-four. I look like I always did. I feel like I always did, except for the not sleeping or eating or peeing and not being able to feel and smell things.

"Fine, then, I'll go to *my* room." And with that Mom turns and leaves.

I start to shiver again. Inside the house feels like outside in winter but when I go to turn up the heat, the thermostat is already at seventy-four.

I hear the sound of a car in the driveway. I run to the window and push open the shade, sure it's Calvin, having come to his senses, but it's only Missy.

"You're back," she says with a sigh of relief. "We were all worried. Let me text Dad that you're okay." She dashes off a message on her phone before turning back to me. "You went to see Calvin?"

I don't bother lying. She always had a Spidey-sense that could see right through me. "Don't tell. Mom already freaked out at me for going anywhere."

"She was really scared when you left. She thought you wouldn't come back."

"She looked at me like she wished I hadn't come back."

"Don't say that."

"Why not? It's true."

"It's not. It's just hard for her to believe you're here. It's a lot to process."

"Dad seems okay. And you hardly blinked."

"That's different," she says.

"How?" I ask but before she can answer, the phone rings. Calvin, I think, but then realize it can't be Calvin because I don't have a phone and we don't have a landline anymore. Missy told me hardly anyone does. And, besides, the ringing is coming from Mom's phone. The caller ID flashes a weirdly familiar name: Peg Weston.

"Is that Dina's mom?" I ask.

Missy grabs the phone and answers it. "Hi, Peg, it's Melissa. Mom left her phone in the kitchen."

My mom was not friendly with Dina's mom even when the two of us were close as kids. I always suspected she felt weird around her because she was a cop. Wait a second! Did she call the freaking cops on me?

I strain to hear what the detective is saying but I can't and Missy's face gives nothing away. "I think she's just having a rough day," Missy says. "You know how it gets around the anniversary." Missy goes quiet as Peg Weston—*Detective* Weston—keeps talking. "I'll tell her," Missy says. "Thanks for being so understanding." More silence. "Yes, give my love to Kathy. Bye."

"What?" I ask after Missy puts down the phone. "Am I in trouble? Is Detective Weston going to, like, arrest me?"

"Of course not."

"Then why is she calling Mom of all people?"

"From what I can gather, Mom called her last night and left a rambling voicemail message worrying that she'd um . . ." Missy pauses and swallows. "Identified the wrong body and asking if there was any DNA left."

"DNA? She called the cops to test my DNA?"

"Not the cops. Just Peg Weston."

"Who's a cop! Who Mom hates!" I grab the phone from Missy and run down the hall to Mom's room, barreling past the closed door. Mom's just sitting there on the bed, staring into space. "Here!" I yank a piece of hair from my head. "You don't believe it's me. Test my DNA."

Mom keeps staring, like I haven't even spoken, like I'm still dead. "Look at me!" I cry, throwing the phone at her. "Don't call the cops. Look at me!"

She won't, though. I rip out another piece of hair and throw it at her. "Look at me," I repeat. "Look at me." I yank out more hair, a fistful this time. I feel the pressure, hear the sound of the follicles snapping, but don't feel any pain.

"Amber, stop it," Missy says, grabbing my hands and pinning them to my sides.

"What the hell?" Dad bursts in just then. He runs to me, grabs my face in his hands, looking at me the way Mom refuses to.

I struggle free and yank out another hunk of hair. I pry open Mom's hand and shove my locks inside it. "You want proof I'm your daughter. Here!"

"Will someone tell me what's going on?" Dad demands.

"Mom called Detective Weston last night. She wants to test my DNA."

"Jesus, Gloria! Why can't you see what's right in front of you?"

"Because, Brian, it can't be."

"But it is," Dad says. "Isn't this what you prayed for every night? And now that you get it, you deny your own daughter."

Mom stares at the hair in her hands and then lets it drop to the floor. "My daughter is dead," she says.

PEG

Thirteen Years Before

Peg Weston knew there were several strikes against her in a town like this: newcomer, police officer, Black, single mother, and now, lesbian. When she was snubbed, as she often was, it wasn't a question of why so much as *which* why.

What had she expected, moving to a place where everyone knew each other and she knew no one, save for a late great-aunt who had unexpectedly left Peg her house? When she'd heard about the bequest, Peg thought she would sell the place. But as the estate moved through probate, her marriage was going through its own death throes. Like her aunt, it had been ill a long time, maybe doomed from the start, predicated as it was on a lie.

When Elijah said that he'd met someone else, Peg felt no rancor. Though it remained mostly unspoken, they were both aware by then that she was gay. "I guess it was obvious," Elijah said when the divorce papers were finalized and they could speak the truth out loud.

"Why? Because I'm a cop?" Peg had asked.

"No. Because I've always repulsed you."

This wasn't true. That she did not desire him did not mean she was disgusted by him. He was, or had been, her friend, and the father of her daughter. It was only after he announced his plans to move across the country with his new, already-pregnant fiancée, leaving their young daughter, that the disgust crept in.

So, there she was, divorced, a single mom, and a newly, kind of, maybe sort-of-out lesbian—she couldn't get used to that word; it sounded like a garden fungus—and the owner of a three-bedroom home with no mortgage. A fresh start seemed in order, so she applied to the squad here and once she was hired, she packed her and Dina's lives into a U-Haul trailer and moved.

She had not expected the welcome wagon, or apple pies left on her doorstep, but she had underestimated how hard it was to make friends at her age. Mothers in the neighborhood gave her tight smiles and a wide berth. Men on the force didn't know what to make of her; aside from Peg, there was only one woman on the force, and she was a rookie uniformed officer. All the other women worked in clerical positions. Maybe there was a gay community in town, but she was not yet ready to figure that all out.

She'd begun to doubt her decision and was considering selling the house when Dina made a friend. A good friend, maybe even a best friend. The two of them played in the front yard almost every day. In the evenings, Dina came home filthy, happy, burbling with stories about this Amber. It was because of Amber that Peg decided to stay.

As fall approached, the weather began to cool, but the girls bundled up in coats and played outside. "You can play inside," Peg told Amber.

"My mom won't let me go into strangers' houses," Amber replied.

Peg was surprised to hear herself considered a stranger but then again she had not spoken to the Cranes more than in passing. She decided to use this as an opportunity to be neighborly, maybe invite the family over. Also to properly explain some of Dina's allergy rules, though Dina knew them fairly well herself.

So on a windy fall day, she walked over and knocked on the Cranes' door. A little girl, perhaps three or four, answered. She wore a suspicious expression and a choppy haircut that looked as though it might have been the result of a craft-scissors experiment.

Peg crouched down to speak eye to eye with her. She was good with children, which was why she was sent to deal with most domestic calls.

"Aren't you a policeman?" the girl asked, even though Peg was not in uniform.

"Close, a policewoman. My name is Detective Weston."

The little girl stared at her with a preternaturally solemn expression. "Where's your badge?"

Peg showed it to her.

"How do I know it's real?"

Peg showed her name, the rank, the details only real badges would have.

The girl's suspicion melted into a gappy smile. "I'm a spy. It's like a detective."

"They're similar," Peg said. "They both require observation and patience."

"Only spies are secret."

"This is true."

The girl stuck out a tiny hand. "I'm Missy."

Enclosing the child's hand in her own, Peg felt an ache inside her. "I'm Margaret. But my friends call me Peg or Peggy."

"What should I call you?"

"That depends; are we friends or colleagues?"

"We are compatriots," the girl said. It was an awfully big word for such a small child, yet Peg felt that it was perfectly apt.

"So, Missy, based on my detective skills, I'm guessing you're Amber's sister."

"You know Amber?"

"Yes. She plays with my daughter, Dina."

Missy frowned. "They won't let me play with them. They say I'm too little."

"Yes, big sisters can be tough that way."

"But they're pretending to be animals. I'm good at pretending."

"Perhaps I can speak to Dina."

Missy shook her head. "It won't help."

She seemed so certain about it, it stretched Peg's heart a little further. "Are your parents home?"

"You won't tell them what I told you about Amber?"

"Of course not."

"Promise?"

"Compatriot's promise."

Her smile broke open her face. It was like a revelation.

"My mom's home but she's in her room with the Do Not Disturb sign up."

"I see," Peg said, the police side of her brain already wondering why Gloria Crane was locked in a room in the middle of the day. She pictured empty booze bottles, neglect. She was thinking this as Gloria emerged into the foyer.

"Detective Weston is here," Missy announced.

Gloria's face seized with panic. Police dropping by unannounced had a tendency to arouse the worst fears.

"Everything's fine," Peg reassured Gloria, something she often needed to do when showing up at people's doors. "I'm not here on official business. I wanted to introduce myself. I'm Margaret Weston. Peg. I'm Dina's mother."

Gloria's shoulders slumped in relief, but now she was the one eyeing Peg suspiciously. Peg noticed the small gold crucifix around her neck. She knew the rumors about herself in town were already circulating. She felt the antipathy coming off this woman.

"The girls have been playing so much and I thought your

family might like to come to dinner one night." Peg had been so keen on the idea before, already imagining the Dina-safe foods she might cook, but now the invitation came out tepid.

"That would be nice." Gloria's reply was equally flat.

They stalled there, the invitation hanging and unwelcome.

"Maybe some weekend coming up," Peg said vaguely.

"Yes. In a few months," Gloria replied. "Things are hectic now. I'm studying for my boards."

"The new year, then," Peg said, certain that this woman would never eat at her table, nor she at hers.

She walked down the path. It was hard living here, hard being simultaneously conspicuous and unseen. Maybe she had made a wrong choice. She fleetingly imagined moving back but it wasn't as if she'd left a full life before. And Dina was happy. Peg could handle being lonely. She was used to it.

Right before she got to the end of the walk, the little girl called out, "Don't forget, we're compatriots," and something in Peg lifted. She had one friend in town, it seemed. Maybe she would be all right here after all.

AMBER

Mom and Dad are fighting. Not arguing as they used to, in hushed tones, behind closed doors, but all-out screaming at each other. Because while Mom had called a cop, Dad had done something even crazier. He'd gone to church.

"I can't believe you!" Mom screams at him. "Now. After all this time!"

"What better time than now?" Dad asks. "I've witnessed a miracle. I wanted to offer thanks."

"It's not a miracle!" Mom shouts back. "Dead people don't come back to life."

"C'mon, Gloria. I've learned a thing or two from you over the years. Scripture's full of miracles. The loaves and fishes? Christ's resurrection?"

"That's the Bible, Brian! And Amber is not Jesus Christ."

"I know that," Dad says. "But she *is* a miracle."

74

I wish he'd stop calling me that. I wish they'd stop fighting. I wish Missy were here, but after Mom got wind of what Dad had done and he got wind of what she'd done, Mom insisted Missy go to work and said tomorrow she had to go back to school. She had perfect attendance and she said the last thing we need now is to draw any suspicion on the family.

They keep going at it. I open the hall closet and take out Mr. Fluff's old daybed, shoving my face in it, imagining him purring on my chest. I bet if he were still alive he'd welcome me back, not deny me or claim I was some kind of second coming.

"I just went to offer thanks, Gloria," Dad says. "I didn't tell anyone. Though I think we should talk to Father Mercer."

"You want to talk to Father Mercer?" The sarcasm in Mom's voice could strip paint. "You always hated him."

"I never hated him. I just wasn't buying what he was selling, and now I see I was wrong to doubt. I think he could help us. Help you."

"Oh, you do, do you?" Mom's not screaming now, she's scoffing, which is somehow worse.

"Who better?" Dad asks. "We should at least approach him."

"Are you insane? We don't even know what's going on, and let's assume for a moment that this is not a hoax or a scam or a communal delusion but is real. A child back from the dead. Can you imagine people's reactions?"

"Yes. People would rejoice in a miracle," Dad says.

"Don't be so naive. At best, it'll be a media circus. Every religious zealot in the world will come out to denounce us or to beatify Amber. And she's not a saint. She is—or was—a perfectly average girl."

This hurts. My mom wasn't the sort to extol Missy or me with superlatives—that was Aunt Pauline's domain—but I always assumed she thought I was special. Apparently not.

"She's a miracle," Dad insists.

"Miracles like this don't happen!"

"What about the Bible? You used to take it at face value."

"I never took it at face value, Brian. I'm not stupid. The whole point of not taking it at face value is that you have faith in a truth beyond what you can see."

"So how is Amber returning not a truth beyond what you can see?"

"Because it's not. The world doesn't work like that."

"Maybe it doesn't until it does. And if Amber's death was God's will, why wouldn't her return also be?"

"I can't have this discussion with you."

"Look, I understand you losing faith when she died, Gloria. I do. But I don't understand you losing it now that she's back."

"You don't get to talk to me about my faith," she sneers.

"Fine. So let's talk to Father Mercer about it." Dad's voice softens. "Let him guide us."

"If this gets out," Mom says in a shout-whisper, "have you thought about what this means for Melissa? That child has been through enough. Her sister died right before her tenth birthday."

That stops me in my tracks. I run back to look at the portrait on the wall and sure enough I died April 28, three days before

76

Missy's birthday. I remember suddenly how she was planning a spy party. God, I was so mean to her about it. About everything. Pauline always said we'd be best friends one day, like she and Mom were, and I guess in the back of my mind, I believed it. Even when I was being horrible to Missy, I thought I'd have time to make it up to her.

Mom's wrong. I wasn't average. I was a shitty person, awful to people who loved me. Why should I get to come back? Why should I get a miracle?

"Melissa will be fine," I hear Dad telling Mom now. "She's the calmest one of all of us."

"And what if people start asking about the money?" Mom asks. "Have you paid it back?"

"Why are you asking me that?"

"I don't know, Brian. Because think of how it looks. Our daughter supposedly dies. The town raises two hundred thousand dollars for a memorial that you spent—"

"We never asked for that money," Dad interrupts.

"That won't matter. We accepted it. And you spent most of it on your ridiculous obsession. And now she's back. Don't you see how this will look?"

"It will look like a miracle."

"It will look like fraud," Mom says.

"I'll pay it back. I don't care about money."

"If you ever loved me at all, Brian," Mom says, her voice almost soft, beseeching, "you will keep this bloody godforsaken miracle to yourself."

CASEY

Seven Years Before

Casey had never felt more like a celebrity than in the weeks following Amber's death. She didn't tell anyone that—of course not—or let it show. In public, she alternated between a somber presence and shuddering sobs, neither of which was contrived. She *was* devastated. She and Amber had been best friends. Amber would have been the first to say so.

This was why the reporter for the local newspaper had gotten in touch with her, not Alexa Santiago or any of Amber's other close friends, but her. She'd been doing a piece about the "tragic hit-and-run accident" that had robbed the town of "one of its brightest lights," the article had said. Before, Casey might've chafed at that designation but now she saw it was true. Amber had been one of those people who was going to go somewhere in life, and Casey had been reflected in her glow. But now Amber was gone and it was like she'd passed on her glow to Casey.

Best friend was how she'd been identified in the smattering of news reports about Amber's death, and it was what was listed on the little text that ran under her name when the local TV news station interviewed her.

The attention had lasted all through the spring and until graduation, when Casey had been selected to give a memorial speech, right alongside the valedictorian. She'd sweated over what to say. There might be reporters there, so it had to be good. She'd also worried about Calvin showing up, even though he'd dropped out of school, the equivalent of fumbling the ball at the three-yard line like the loser that he was.

She'd spent hours working on the speech, googling quotes about death. Her favorite one was by George Eliot: *Our dead are never dead to us until we have forgotten them.* She'd made the mistake of calling George a him when she turned out to be a woman, but whatever. "I will never forget Amber," she said at the start of her speech, and then went on to paint a picture of the most beautiful friendship in the world. She got so swept up in it that she cried, missing Amber, and missing the relationship she'd described.

After graduation, things went, more or less, back to normal. The flowers and teddy bears that had been piled at the four-way stop where Amber had been struck were bagged up and removed. A few weeks later, someone locked a spray-painted white bicycle to the lamppost as a memorial (a creepy one, if you asked Casey). The TV crews left; the articles dwindled and disappeared altogether. The people who had rushed to Casey's side, supporting the grieving best friend, stopped leaving her self-care gifts like bath bombs and went back to the business of pool parties and shopping for sheets for their college dorms.

It was around this time that Casey had the idea for the memorial fund. She would single-handedly raise money for the Crane family, who, she knew, while not poor, were definitely not rich. Instead of going on nice vacations like Casey's family did—usually to a Caribbean resort in winter and somewhere in Europe in summer—Amber's family often just went camping. Instead of the elaborate sweet sixteen at the country club that Casey had been thrown, Amber's party had been in her backyard. She didn't get a new car when she got her license as Casey had, or even a used one. She continued to ride that bicycle everywhere. Sometimes, when it seemed like Amber had everything—a boyfriend who loved her, parents who paid attention to her, even a sibling, though Amber complained constantly about Missy—Casey would compare her life to Amber's to remind herself that Casey had it as good, if not better.

But now such comparisons were moot. And Casey wanted to continue honoring her friend. So, she put up a bunch of pictures of her and Amber through the years, cribbed the best lines from her speech, and set up a fundraising page to, she explained, "help the Crane family through their darkest hour." She was worried people would be mean about it. It wasn't like they could buy Amber back, but the morning after the post had gone up, Casey had raised over a thousand dollars. In addition to the money were messages, some from people who hadn't even known Amber and had never met Casey, blessing them both.

She reached out to the reporter at the local paper who had interviewed her to tell her about the fund. The reporter was interested in what she called "the new trend of crowdsourcing tragedy." She did an article, not about Casey, but about the money she'd raised, which by that time had jumped to $20,000. When the article came out, the donations swelled to $65,000, then $100,000.

Casey emailed the article to every person in her contacts. She asked people to forward the article along with the link to the fund to everyone they knew. Complete strangers emailed her back, saying they'd donated, extolling Casey for being a wonderful friend to Amber first in life, and now in death. One lady from Missoula, Montana, called Casey "an angel on earth." Casey's heart had swelled. She could not bring Amber back, but she could bring some solace to her family. And to herself.

Until she got the message from Calvin, who she must have accidentally included in her mass email. She hadn't heard from him since the day Amber died; she was beginning to convince herself that he'd never existed.

What the HELL are you doing? he wrote. Why are you raising all this money? The funeral already happened and if you think this changes anything, you're wrong. Money can't erase what we did.

She deleted the email but it was too late. It all came crashing back, and she started to cry, only it wasn't that cathartic good sob she'd done in front of the camera, or on the graduation stage. It was an ugly cry, in all the ways.

Her father happened to come upon her like this. He was not much of a hugger. He'd said more than once that girls were too touchy-feely and would do better in business if they grew a thicker skin. But when he saw her, he wrapped his arms around her and asked: "Princess, what's wrong?"

"It's . . . it's Amber," she hiccuped.

"Oh, sweetheart," he said, pulling her into his lap, like she was a little girl.

After she stopped crying, her father asked her how much money the fund had raised. He'd been very impressed with Casey's initiative and had even asked his assistant to create a computer graphic that grew as the funds did.

"One hundred and eighty-seven thousand dollars," she told him.

"Wow! And where is the money?"

She wasn't entirely sure how that part worked. It was still in the computer as far as she knew. The Cranes would have to fill out some paperwork to access it.

"Let's go over there now," her father said. "And tell the family about the amazing thing you've done for them. That will make you feel better."

And so they'd driven over to Amber's house and knocked on the door. Amber's dad answered, though he didn't look like the Mr. Crane Casey remembered, who was like a TV dad, always full of goofy jokes and smiles. This man had unkempt hair and bloodshot eyes and a big stain on his shirt.

"Yes?" He stared at Casey as if she was a stranger, not his daughter's best friend.

"Mr. Crane. It's me, Casey," she began, but something about the look in his eyes stopped her.

Her father took over, shaking hands with Mr. Crane, re-introducing himself.

"Right, Scott, Casey, sorry, I'm not quite myself. What can I do for you?"

"I'm sure you're aware that my daughter has been raising money for your family in the aftermath of your daughter's passing."

It had been in the newspaper and all over social media, but Mr. Crane looked as if he were hearing it for the first time.

"She raised nearly two hundred thousand dollars for your time of need," Casey's father elaborated.

Casey waited for Mr. Crane to smile, or even cry or jump for joy, as she would have if someone announced they were giving her that much money. It was like winning the lottery without even buying a ticket. But Mr. Crane just stared and asked, "Why?"

"To help with expenses," Casey said.

"The funeral must have set you back a pretty penny," Casey's father said, his voice tight, the way it was when he fought with Casey's mother. "And now you can set up a memorial for Amber. Maybe even a scholarship in her name at the school. A way to honor her legacy."

"Oh," Mr. Crane said. He still did not seem terribly happy

about it. "Thank you." He started to close the door, but Casey's father shoved his foot in it.

"'*Thank you*'? Is that all you have to say? Do you have any idea of the effort my daughter put into this?"

Mr. Crane seemed to wince at the mention of the word *daughter,* and in that moment, Casey had the briefest sense of what it would feel like to lose a child, the ineffable and unending well of grief.

"It's okay, Dad." Casey pulled at his sleeve, suddenly wanting to be anywhere but here.

"It's not okay. We all suffer in life. That doesn't mean we can treat one another with disrespect."

"Really, Dad! It's okay."

Her father turned to her, angry, not at Mr. Crane anymore but at her. She shrank back, the tears welling in her eyes having nothing to do with Amber.

"No, your father's right," Mr. Crane replied. He looked to be blinking back his own tears. "Thank you, Casey. Thank you for being such a good friend to Amber in life, and in death."

She felt bile rise in her throat, choking her, making her unable to speak. Mr. Crane reached forward and hugged her and the most horrible sob escaped. Mr. Crane and her father thought that she was crying because she missed Amber, and she let them think that. But really, she was missing a part of herself that she wasn't sure had ever existed.

AMBER

Someone is knocking at my window. It doesn't quite wake me—because whatever it is that I do at night now doesn't seem to be sleeping—but it rouses me. I glance at the clock. It's 11:37.

I'm still hoping it's Calvin. He's had time to get over the shock, to believe that I'm really back, and will take me in his arms and I'll be able to feel it, feel him.

It's not Calvin. I can tell as soon as I open the window, even though it's too dark to make out more than an outline of a person. Which means a stranger is at my window. I start to close it but someone's hand is already lodged there. "Hey," it cries as I slam the jamb down.

I recognize the voice, fluty and mellifluous, capable of doing the best animal impressions: duck, cow, horse, pig.

I open the window and there is Dina Weston, examining her smashed hand.

"Oh my God, Dina! Are you okay?"

Dina shakes out her hand. "I appear to be just fine."

I open the window all the way. For a minute, we just stare at each other. When we were little, we invented this game we called UC Farm where we would spend hours on end pretending to be animals, never uttering a word, but somehow communicating just fine. We have not played that in years but it seems like we have not forgotten how to communicate in silence.

"It's good to see you, Amber," she says at last. "Really good."

"It's good to see you, too." And it is. Even though Dina and I drifted apart years before I died.

"I guess my mom spilled everything to your mom," I say, trying to hide my annoyance. Such a hypocrite! After Mom and Dad finished fighting earlier, Dad sat me down for a talk. He told me I wasn't to see anyone. I wasn't to go anywhere. I wasn't to communicate with anyone. "Until we get this sorted. It's too confusing to explain to people," he said, and I could tell it was Mom's words he was parroting. Mom who told Peg Weston, who clearly told Dina. Still, I'm so happy to see Dina, I let it slide.

"Your mom and mine talk a lot these days," Dina says.

"But they used to hate each other."

"No. Your mom hated my mom," Dina corrected. I wait for her to add something along the lines of, *like you hated me.* But she doesn't. Because that is all water under the bridge now. And anyhow, I never actually hated Dina. "I think they're really good friends now."

"When did that happen?" I ask.

"Maybe a few years ago."

"Weird."

"Weirder than this?" Dina zigs a hand back and forth between us.

"Fair point," I say.

The wind rattles in the window. "Come in, it's cold out." Only the weird thing is, it's not cold, or I don't feel it. For the first time, I'm not freezing. I gesture for Dina to come inside. She plunks down on my bed and pulls down the hood from the sweatshirt she's wearing, emblazoned with the name of the college she must have gone to. Except for her hair, which she always wore in long braids but now has down in soft curls, she looks pretty much the same as she did when I last saw her.

"What have you been up to? Did you finish college? Study zoology? Did you go out West?" I say, remembering how when she was little, Dina spoke endlessly of moving closer to her dad, who lived on the West Coast with his new wife and their kids—Dina's half siblings who she'd seen only on a handful of Christmases.

"Not yet." She seems bummed about it, which makes sense given how her dad basically dumped her for a new family, so I don't probe further. "What have you been up to?"

"Not much. I'm under house arrest. My parents are freaked out."

Dina plays with her bracelets, a bunch of those rubber bangles she always wore to hide the MedicAlert band, which she hated. "That's understandable. It's a lot to take in."

"They've gone all prison warden on me because I left the

house." I pause, deciding to trust Dina. "I went to see Calvin."

"He *saw* you?"

"Totally. Though I barely recognized him. I mean, he looked terrible, so withered and skinny, but now that I'm back, I've been thinking that I can help him get better." As I say it, I begin to wonder if *this* was why I couldn't feel him kissing me. Because he couldn't feel it, wouldn't allow himself to feel it. Same as Mom. Maybe that's why I'm cold around them. They haven't let me back in. Maybe when they do, I'll be hungry again. I'll sleep again. I'll be warm again. I'll be fully alive again.

Suddenly, the need to see Calvin is even more urgent. I need to save him. To save me. To save us.

"Do you know where he lives? If he's with anyone? My sister didn't think so but she wasn't sure."

Dina shrugs. "How would I know any of that?"

Dina and Calvin didn't exactly run in the same crowd. I don't know if they even knew each other. Still, maybe they became friends after I died. If Mom and Peggy Weston did, anything's possible.

"I actually thought you were Calvin just now, that he'd gotten over the shock of it." Dina's face falls so I hastily add, "But I'm so glad it's you."

She fiddles with her bracelets. "Thanks."

"It might take him more time to accept it," I say. "To accept me."

"Yeah," Dina agrees. "Some things take time."

"I know. But on the other hand, we've already lost seven

years. And I'm still in love with him. Do you think he could be in love with me? We were supposed to be forever."

"I don't know," she admits.

"Sorry, I'm only talking about me. I've barely asked about you. What's new?"

She shrugs. "Not much to tell. I'm the same . . ." She drifts off.

"As you ever were," I finish. "Because people stay their essential selves. Like I'm still me and Calvin is still him." I pause. "Right?"

Dina gets this look on her face, her eyes turned up, her chin quivering. "What? Do you know something?"

She doesn't say anything.

"Dina! I know you know! You could never keep a secret. Remember that time you got to take home the class rabbit even though you weren't supposed to have animals? You were going to hide it in your room to keep it from your mom. You lasted like ten minutes."

"Because I started sneezing." She pauses. "But this isn't a secret. Everyone knows."

"Knows what?"

"About your dad."

"What about him?"

"He's convinced Calvin was responsible."

"Responsible for what?"

Dina looks up and stares me right in the face. "For your death, Amber."

"What are you talking about?"

89

"The police never found out who the driver was. No cameras, no witnesses. My mom worked the case for months. But all the leads dried up. Your dad, though, he got it stuck in his head that it was Calvin. He hired an investigator and everything. It got pretty ugly for a while. Really divided the town."

"Calvin! He would never hurt me. He loved me. Why would my father think that?"

Dina shrugs. "My mom says grief makes people crazy."

"Poor Calvin. No wonder he got so lost." I pause, knowing I have no right to ask this of Dina, but she's the only one I can ask. "Will you go see him for me?"

"Me?"

"I'm under house arrest and clearly seeing me is too much for him. But you. You won't freak him out. He knew we were good friends once. Best friends."

"He did?" Dina sounds so hopeful that I don't tell her that he only found that out when we were looking at old photos of me and he came across a photo of the Halloween when Dina and I went as a cheetah and an elephant.

"Yes. You can convince him. Tell him it's really me. I'm here. And I know he would never do anything to hurt me."

Dina hesitates as she runs her finger up and back along her MedicAlert bracelet. "I'm not sure he'll hear that from me."

"He will! You've known me longer than anyone. And you believe I'm back. You could vouch for me. We used to be best friends once. That has to count for something."

She meets my gaze straight on. Her eyes are a greenish

gold—like a lion's, she used to say. When we were younger, she really wanted to be an animal. So did I, but I grew out of it, grew out of her, basically dumped her to hang out with Casey and Alexa. So I know I don't have any right to ask her this. But she's here. She came to see me. That has to mean something.

She stares at me a moment longer and then she puts up the hood. "I'll see what I can do."

"Thank you! Thank you!" I hug Dina. She was always slight but now she's practically nothing, a wisp of a person.

"When you see him, tell him," I exhort her as she climbs through the window.

"Tell him what?"

"That I forever love him."

CALVIN

Eight Years Before

Calvin was always scared that he would hurt Amber. The first time he'd kissed her, the day after Lee Franklin's party, he'd held her face in his hands, felt that fragile jawbone, beating a pulse so strong. A hummingbird in a bear claw.

The night before, they'd talked while the party raged around them. She had a midnight curfew, so he'd walked her home, even though she had a bike and he had his mom's car. He was in the street, wheeling her bike; she was on the curb and still he towered over her.

When they got to her house, he hadn't known what to do. He wanted to kiss her but he didn't dare press his luck. A light illuminated one of the rooms and Calvin suspected someone was waiting up for her.

"I'm working a bake sale tomorrow for the musical," Amber said, pausing before her front walk. "Come see me?"

He'd been so grateful for the invitation, the promise of continuation, he'd forgotten to ask where the bake sale was. The next day he had to suffer the indignity of asking Dean to ask Amber's friend Alexa, though he knew this would mean Dean meowing at him for several more weeks.

The bake sale was at the park next to the rec center. A series of tables overflowing with brownies and cupcakes and Rice Krispies Treats run by the drama kids. He held back a minute and just watched Amber interact with the customers, smiling as she made change. Everyone who spoke to her smiled and laughed back, like they were sprinkled with a bit of her magic.

And then she saw him, standing behind the white oak tree, and she smiled at him. And with that, he was a goner.

She motioned for him to wait under the tree, which was just starting to turn an orangish color. An amber color. It felt like a sign. After a few minutes, she trotted over bearing a Rice Krispies Treat, and though Calvin didn't like marshmallows, he'd swallowed it in two bites.

They talked for a bit, about this and that—he couldn't remember the specifics—before she said she had to get back to work.

"Okay," he said, devastated, like he'd blown his opportunity.

But then Amber smiled once more and said, "Aren't you going to kiss me goodbye?"

When Calvin kissed her, he tasted marshmallows and marveled at the way his life had changed overnight. He felt the flutter of the vein in her cheek. *Hummingbird,* he thought. He circled her entire neck with his one hand, feeling the pulse hammer against him.

"You're choking me a bit," she said.

"Oh. God. I'm so sorry." He hadn't realized what he had done. He was mortified once again by his bulk.

"It's okay." She took her hand, put it up against his. It was half the size.

"I'm too big."

"And I'm too small," she said. "If we ever have kids, they'll be just right." She blushed when she said that, looked away. Calvin felt magic again. But entwined with it, fear. That he might hurt her if he weren't careful.

He carried that fear with him no matter how many times she told him: "You're not going to hurt me." She said it that afternoon at the bake sale, and again a few weeks later when they were fooling around in the back of his mom's car, where the ill fit of his XXL body and her petite one were not helped by the squished dimensions of the hatchback. And again when Amber announced she was ready to have sex and wanted them to do it after junior prom, Calvin felt that fear all over again. Never mind that he knew her family would disapprove, the physics of it scared him, the bulk of him, the slightness of her.

"I'm not as breakable as I look," she told him.

This he knew. She might have been a foot shorter and much, much lighter but in most ways that counted, Amber was tougher than him. She knew her mind. And when she decided something, she decided, and there was no arguing, only going along for the ride.

When she didn't speak of having sex again, he half hoped she'd forget about it, half prayed that she wouldn't. After the limo they'd rented with all her friends stopped outside her house and he'd pinned the corsage on her—an arrangement that along with the rented tux and their share of the limo cost a week's wages—she'd whispered in his ear, "I don't have to be home until morning." She opened her clutch purse and showed him the shiny foil condom wrappers inside. "I reserved us a hotel room."

The dance felt like a month of Sundays, dragging on and on. Calvin did not remember a single thing about it. All he could think about was those condoms, that hotel room. They went to the after-party, holding hands. He had to hide his boner with a throw pillow.

It got late. He wondered if she'd changed her mind. It was okay if she had. He might even be relieved.

But then she whispered in his ear: "Ready to go?"

She had booked a room in the Red Lion Inn. It cost $150 a night. He tried to give her money but she said it was on her.

When they registered, he couldn't bear to look at the clerk. He kept feeling like someone was going to catch him for something. But the guy just activated a key card and said that checkout was at eleven.

Inside the room, Amber flicked on the lamp. She had brought a bottle of sparkling cider and she poured it into the hotel glasses, which were nice, not plastic like the ones at the motels they stayed at on wrestling meets.

"Should we get undressed now?" Amber asked after they toasted each other and forever love.

Calvin hesitated.

"Don't you want to?"

So bad he was bursting with it. "I don't want to crush you," he confessed.

Standing on tippy-toes, she reached up to wrap her arms around his neck. He bent his head down to meet her. "What if I like being crushed by you?" she whispered, the soft sibilants in his ear doing crazy things to him.

She started to pull the straps off her shoulders.

"Wait," he said. The corsage he had bought her was a waterfall of flowers, amaranths the florist had recommended, unusual, and they would dry nicer than roses. "So your true love will have a keepsake," she'd said.

He unpinned the corsage, his hands shaking. "I don't want this to get messed up."

She stood on her tippy-toes again and kissed him. Calvin tasted marshmallows, as he did every time he kissed her.

"I forever love you, Calvin Judd," she said.

It wasn't the first time they had said the words to each other. But it was the first time Calvin felt the weight of loving someone. Of being loved. It was bigger than anything in his life.

"I forever love you, too, Amber Crane," Calvin replied.

AMBER

In the name of keeping up appearances, Mom and Dad declare that everyone should act as if everything is normal. They both will go to work. Missy will go to school. "And I keep being dead?" I complain.

Mom shoots me daggers.

"What? Too soon?"

"I'll be home after school," Missy promises.

"No, you have work today," Mom replies. "You should go."

"Where do you work?" I ask. Of all the things I can't quite wrap my head around, my sister being a teenager is the hardest. She's not Missy anymore. She's Melissa. She's almost the same age as I was when I died.

"At a thrift store."

"Explains the wardrobe," I quip, and stop myself. The habit of teasing Missy—no, Melissa—is hardwired in me. "Sorry."

"Why?" she asks. "It's funny and true." She gathers up her jacket, the kind of thing someone at a service station would wear. "See?"

I nod. "It's kind of cool," I say. "You're kind of cool."

"I know, right?" she says with a smile. "You can use any of my things while I'm gone. Since you don't have any things. My computer is on."

"I'll skip the clothes but maybe take you up on the computer."

"I'll pick up some new clothes for you but you are not to communicate with anyone!" Mom exhorts. "No phone calls or emails or any online chatting."

As soon as they leave, I fire up Melissa's computer to get a hold of Dina. Technically, this is against the rules, but Dina already knows about me because Mom broke the rules, so it feels like a wash.

Melissa's computer has a program open, the social media application everyone is using now, I assume, so I search for Dina and pull up a dozen Dina Westons that aren't her. Which tracks. Dina was never one to follow a trend. It wouldn't surprise me if she didn't have any accounts.

I try searching for Calvin on the app but find nothing. I have more luck with my old best friend, Casey, who's very active, posting a ton of pictures. Unlike Dina, she looks older, her hair now blond instead of brown, but she still has that same bright, let's-party grin on display in the multiple shots of her at bars with other girls who look like her. Casey's still Casey, I think.

She used to say she could have fun at a wake.

After a few pages of Casey-in-bars shots, I try Alexa Santiago's page. If Casey was the party girl, Alexa was the serious one. I was in between. Casey used to call me the glue. I wonder what happened when the glue went away.

Alexa is far less active online than Casey. From what I can tell, she's in law school, and is engaged. She hardly posted in college, so I switch to the site everyone used when we were in high school where I find a few posts from college, some really nice ones about me after I died, and then before that, posts that I remember.

Deep into her feed, I find a picture of Calvin and me that I've never seen before. Casey was the one who apparently took it and she tagged Alexa but not me. *How much do you love this pic of Cal*, Casey wrote. Which is weird because no one called him Cal except his mom. And again, weird because she didn't tag me. And weirdest yet that she was complimenting him. She thought Calvin was basic and dumb. She used to secretly call him the Meat Puppet.

As I keep scrolling, I find a picture of all of us from junior prom taken inside the rented limo. And before that, the picture of Calvin pinning the corsage to me. *Prom king and queen?* Alexa had written in the caption, even though Fiona Tucker and Nolan Sacks won that year. *More like Beauty and the Beast,* Casey wrote in the comments. And beneath that in a separate comment. *JK.*

I remember when Calvin pinned the corsage on me that

night. And later that night, I remember when he removed it. His hands had trembled both times. "I don't want to hurt you," he'd said. And I had told him that he didn't need to worry. He could never hurt me. How could my father think that he could?

I type in my name and click on the news icon.

There are a bunch of articles. The digital version of my obituary. One about the hit-and-run and another about crowd-sourcing trauma, with a quote from Casey, who I guess raised all that money for my family that I'd heard Mom and Dad arguing about. There's another big *National Geographic* article about the white-bicycle memorials, bikes spray-painted white and stationed where there was a bicycle-related fatality. I guess someone made one for me, according to the article.

And then I get to this article.

"A Father's Crusade," reads the headline. There's a grainy photo of Dad holding an even grainier picture of me. *Brian Crane vows to keep looking for the driver who struck and killed his daughter*, reads the caption.

The article itself is as much about the investigation into the accident that caused my death as it is about Dad. It discusses the forensic evidence, or lack thereof, taken from the scene. The tire skid marks were identified but it was a "ubiquitous" brand of tire. There were no paint scratches found on my bike, and though investigators distributed swatches of my bike's unusual shade to auto body shops within a five-hundred-mile radius, asking mechanics to notify them if any car had scratches with such paint, this led nowhere.

The police had pursued the possibility that the accident was intentional but had ruled that out. There was a quote from Detective Weston: "Amber Crane was not just a member of our community, she was a family friend. The department is pursuing all possible leads to solve this tragic accident, but hit-and-runs are notoriously difficult. Sadly, only about ten percent of such perpetrators are ever caught. That said, the investigation is ongoing and we've set up a tip line for people to report any and all leads."

The article then pivots to Dad. How he didn't believe the police had done enough. How he had hired a private investigator to look into theories that were, in his words, "unpopular with local law enforcement but nevertheless very feasible." He pledged he would not stop his crusade until the driver was found. He had taken out a full-page ad in several local newspapers asking for leads, had even rented a billboard. "This is my promise to my daughter. It's a promise I won't break as long as I live."

I can't help thinking of how the old me would feel about all this. I was a little famous. In a national magazine, even. But seeing this now it's so clear that my life had really amounted to nothing. The only thing notable about me was that I died. And now even that's up for debate.

ARNOLD

Six Years Before

Anyone who taught high school long enough would witness a few deaths. It was the age, really. Teenagers. Prime time for risk-taking. Unfinished prefrontal cortexes. A misguided sense of invincibility. Arnold had read the studies showing spiked mortality rates for young adults. Over the years, he'd attended a number of student funerals. Adam DeJesus, car accident. Nicola Hynes, drowning. Hayley Fetterman, suicide. Peter Alston, cancer.

It came with the territory, so Arnold wasn't entirely sure why Amber Crane's death should linger.

It was probably his age. At sixty-five, he understood mortality in a way that he had not before. The hourglass was emptying, and his time was on the ebb now. He couldn't help feeling that he'd wasted so much of it. Seeing a seventeen-year-old robbed of the life in front of her hammered that home.

His biggest regret was that he had no family. He'd always

thought he would have a large one and had been married when he was young, but the relationship had fallen apart in less than a year and he'd never married again.

His students had come to be his children, at least for the fifty minutes a day he had them. Mostly they treated him with a casual disdain that he knew not to take personally. Occasionally, however, a student would reach out to him for some kind of help. It was these moments that Arnold lived for.

Which was maybe another reason he could not stop thinking about Amber.

Late last year, Calvin Judd had requested a letter of recommendation. Arnold had asked him what schools he was applying to and Calvin had named a few decent colleges in state, and one out of state. "That's quite a good school," Arnold had said.

"I know," the young man had replied. "But I might not get in."

"And you also might get in."

"It's far away."

"Lots of young people go away for college."

"Yeah, but my girlfriend is going to school here. She wants to stay close to her family."

Arnold knew that his girlfriend was Amber Crane. They had both been his students. He had seen them around campus, holding hands. They made a sweet couple, she so slight, he so substantial. Watching them filled him with a sort of unease. Maybe it was that at sixteen those two had something he never had. Or maybe there was something slightly suspect about spying on teenage children.

He had agreed to write Calvin a letter of recommendation (particularly after he had looked up Calvin's record and been happily surprised to see he had been an admirable student, overcoming a learning disability).

When Calvin was accepted to the out-of-state school, he had come to Arnold to share the news and seek counsel. He still had not told his girlfriend that he'd applied. He didn't even know why he'd applied. The school was so expensive and far away. What should he do?

Arnold advised him to await the financial aid offer before making any decision, but reminded him that whatever he chose, true love would wait. (As if he had any experience with this.)

Months later, after the Crane girl died, and Arnold learned that not only had Calvin not gone to the out-of-state school, but he had also dropped out of Kennedy High five weeks prior to graduation, he had been sorely upset.

Maybe that was part of the reason he was stuck on the Crane girl. He somehow felt complicit in her death. He couldn't stop thinking about the obituary assignment he had failed her on. If he could have, he would have retroactively amended her grade. Because her obituary had turned out to be the most prophetic of the lot. She'd never had the chance to live her dream life.

Unlike most teachers, Arnold dreaded the summer, when the yawning quiet of his daily routine became nearly unbearable. He usually completed a large home-improvement project to occupy his time: a new roof; a new deck; last summer he'd replaced his house's siding. But the summer after Amber died, he could not face being home alone with his thoughts.

So he began his drives. Each day, he ventured farther—two, three hours, sometimes longer. He had no destination in mind. He was happy to be lost.

He'd lived in the same town for more than forty years, but his life was circumscribed by school and home. Which was maybe why out on the drives, he discovered things that had been there all along, only invisible to him.

He did not know there was a farm stand at McBurney Farm where one could buy peaches so fresh off the tree that they were warm, as if bearing sunshine in their flesh. He had never noticed the baseball diamond carved into a ring of trees near the butte. It seemed fantastical, like in that movie where Kevin Costner built a ball field in the midst of all that corn.

There was a diner twenty miles out of town that served a variety of fresh pies. The waitress's name was Rhetta. He stopped in twice that first summer, and when he returned this year, Rhetta still knew his order and still called him "honey." She was at least twenty years younger than him, so he had no illusions, but it felt good to be remembered.

Every day, he discovered something new.

Today, for instance, he had found the bicycle, chained to the lamppost out at the four-way stop on Summit. He had driven past it any number of times but noticed it today only because someone was photographing it.

Before, Arnold would not have interrupted a stranger. But today, he got out of his car, staying a respectful distance from the man with the camera until the man called out a welcoming "Hello."

"Don't want to interrupt you," Arnold said.

"That's okay. The light is dying."

He approached the young man, who appeared to be in his midthirties, young enough and familiar enough to have been one of Arnold's students, though he couldn't place him. The man was squatting in front of the bicycle, which he now saw wasn't a working bicycle.

"It's called a ghost bike," the man said.

"What's it's for?" Arnold asked.

"It commemorates people killed in bike accidents. They're popping up all over the country, as memorials but also as a warning to drivers to slow down, to look what can happen."

"It's rather . . . ghostly," Arnold said.

"It does feel a little bit sacred," the man said. "I've been coming here for the last few weeks to photograph it. I have this wild plan to go shoot other ghost bikes. Try to do a feature on them for someone." He made a face. "Does that make me sound morbid?"

"Not morbid at all," Arnold replied. "Just curious."

"I am curious. There's a Filipino saying that someone has itchy feet, meaning they have wanderlust. My lola used to say I have itchy feet and an itchy brain because I want to go everywhere, see everything."

"Itchy feet and brain sound like excellent qualities."

The man chuckled, then was quiet for a long time before he smiled. "I appreciate you saying so."

"I knew the girl on the bike," Arnold told the man. "She was a student of mine at Kennedy."

"Really?" the man said. "Maybe I've shot her. I do school pictures there."

"Ah, so you're a photographer, then?" That explained his familiarity.

"I'd hardly call it that. I wanted to be one. A photojournalist, really, but I'm not."

"Not *yet*," Arnold corrected. "How old are you?"

"Thirty-four," the young man said.

"Still plenty of time," Arnold said. "I expect that one day I'll see you in print. Tell me your name so I'll know it when I see it."

"Nick Flores."

Arnold took out the marking pen he kept on him at all times, even in the summer, and on a scrap of paper from his pocket wrote down the name.

"One day, Nick Flores, I will see your byline. I just know it." He had no idea if this was true, but from years of teaching he knew that sometimes you had to help students see a bigger future for themselves. It was the entire reason behind the obituary assignment.

Nick was quiet for another moment. Then he asked, "What was the name of the student?"

"Amber," Arnold said. "Amber Crane."

"Amber Crane," Nick repeated. "Thank you."

The sun was dipping below the horizon, the white bicycle a beacon somehow in the golden light.

Arnold got back in his car, waiting to see where the road would take him next.

AMBER

I'm pacing, waiting for Dad to come home so I can confront him about Calvin, but he's still at work and Melissa's still at school. I thought Mom had gone to work, too, but she came home after only a few hours with a bag full of new clothes that she dumped in front of me before leaving again. The entire transaction happened without her looking at me, never mind hugging me or doing typical mom stuff. If anything, she seems mad at me. Mad that I died. Mad that I didn't. I can't tell the difference.

When Melissa finally comes in at five o'clock, I practically pounce on her. "I'm so glad you're here!" I say before she even takes off her gas-station-attendant jacket. "I missed you."

She pauses, smiling as she hangs up the jacket in the front-hall closet.

"What's funny?" I ask.

"You missed me," she says. "It's nice to hear."

"Well, did *you* miss *me*?"

Melissa looks at me squarely. There's something about her expression that feels so grown-up, way more adult than I was at seventeen. "Yes and no," she says.

"Ouch," I say, even though I think she's joking. Though she would have every reason not to miss me. I was such a bitch to her.

I follow her to the kitchen. She opens the refrigerator and pulls out a hunk of cheese and an apple, and then goes to the pantry for some crackers before sitting down at the kitchen table. I plunk down across from her. I look at the cheese, crumbly sharp cheddar Mom always bought, and the apple, small and green and glistening, appetizing, and yet I can't even imagine putting them in my mouth, chewing, swallowing.

"I don't seem to eat," I confess to Melissa because I need to tell someone. "I don't know why. It's not exactly something you can look up on WebMD. But maybe it's like my systems have to reboot." I pause. "Don't tell."

"I won't," she says. "Anyhow, I already knew."

"How?"

"I pay attention, Amber. I've always paid attention."

"Once a spy, always a spy." I pause. "And you haven't already told Mom and Dad?"

"No. Why would I?"

"You used to be so terrible at keeping secrets."

Melissa gives me a peculiar look as she peels the apple skin

109

in one long strip. "I was *great* at keeping secrets. It was my specialty."

"You went around spying on people."

Melissa cuts a slice of apple and a piece of cheese and layers them on a cracker. "I know, but I never told anyone what I saw."

"What was the point of spying if you didn't tell?"

"I was looking for answers," she replies, popping the cheese, apple, and cracker into her mouth. "For myself."

"Did you find them?"

She chews, swallows, and grins. Suddenly I can see my little sister, excitedly telling me how she'd figured out what I was getting for my thirteenth birthday present or whispering that Dad had found out about me and Calvin "doing it" and later yet inviting me to her spy party. She was so sweet and open but I shot her down every time.

"I did." She makes another cracker, cheese, and apple sandwich, eating it with relish before she adds, "I did miss you today. I hated being away. I just wanted to come back and be with you."

"Why?" My voice is tart, verging on mean, a tone that would have been very familiar to nine-year-old Missy. Only this time, my disdain is aimed squarely at myself.

"Why?" she repeats, pushing her plate back. "Because you're my sister."

"Yeah. A shitty sister. I made fun of you. I excluded you. I treated you like crap."

Melissa carries her plate to the sink, rinsing it and putting it in the dishwasher. With her back to me, she says, "That was a long time ago. Things change. People change."

"But I didn't. I died an asshole."

Melissa shrugs. "I didn't see it that way."

"It doesn't matter how you saw it. It's a fact." I pause. "I was not a good sister."

"You were!"

"I wasn't. I knew I wasn't. I always figured we'd get close when we were older, like Mom and Pauline. That I'd have time to fix it."

"And you did."

"As far as I can see, I only screwed things up worse." I sigh. "I mean, Mom and Dad split up. I didn't think there was a force on earth that could do that."

"That's not your fault," Melissa says.

"Kind of is. Even if it isn't."

As Melissa wraps the cheese in plastic, not messily as I would, but carefully, like it's a gift, I ask: "What happened with them? Was it because of religion?" That had always been a bone of contention between them, but their fights were more like debates, with neither side ever conceding.

Melissa pauses. "I don't think it helped when Dad punched a guy in church."

"Shut up! He did not!"

"He did. Some well-meaning parishioner told Dad that you dying was God's will. We heard this a lot. But I guess it was one time too many. Dad just lost it and clocked the guy, broke his nose."

111

"Oh, shit." I start to laugh. "I know I'll probably go to hell for saying this, but I wish I could have seen that." I pause. "Or maybe this is hell. Do you think this is hell?"

"I don't believe in hell," Melissa says. "It's just a construct, a way of controlling people, the way parents threaten time-outs if you don't eat your vegetables. And you being back is a gift. So, definitely not hell."

"What happened after Dad punched the parishioner? Mom got pissed and they split up?"

"That was just one of a thousand cuts. When Mr. Fluff died, Mom completely lost it. She was dry-eyed at your funeral, in a daze—like she is now. Everyone said she was in shock, but I think it was something else. Like she just couldn't touch the pain. But the cat died. Officially he ran away, but he'd been sick and the vet said cats often disappear outside to die. We never found him and Mom went bonkers for a while. She checked all the animal shelters once, sometimes twice a day, looking for him. She cried so hard, her jaw started clicking. Dad couldn't believe that she was going to all this trouble to find a cat that was obviously dead but was no help trying to find who killed you."

"'A Father's Crusade.'" I repeat the headline of the article.

"You know about that?"

I nod. "I may have researched myself."

"Well, yeah, that was a big wedge, too. Mom was mad that he wouldn't let it go, but he kept pushing, taking out ads, a billboard even, hiring a series of private detectives, spending all this money. Mom begged him to stop but he wouldn't. It's ironic, though."

"What is?"

"Mom searching the pet shelters for Mr. Fluff, Dad trying to find your 'killer.'" She makes air quotes around the word *killer*. "Both of them were, in their way, searching for you."

"When did you get so damn insightful?"

Melissa shrugged. "I told you. I paid attention."

"Maybe I should've paid more attention."

"It's never too late."

"Except sometimes it is."

Mom's car pulls into the driveway and screeches to a halt. The door slams shut. I can tell from here that she's enraged—still, or again—and I wonder how I messed up this time.

She flings open the door and my mother, who used to teach catechism because she enjoyed it, who never cursed or raised her voice or took the Lord's name in vain or even said "God," the way some people do as an expletive, shouts: "Where the fuck is he? Where the fuck is your goddamn father?"

"He's not here," I say, suddenly worried about my dad. "What did he do?"

"He told . . ." Mom's voice shakes with anger. "He told Father Mercer."

BRIAN
Five Years Before

"Why?" Gloria asked.

It was a question his wife had not stopped asking in the two years since the hospital called and told them there'd been an accident. Amber was already gone, DOA by the time the ambulance reached her, but the hospital wouldn't tell you that over the phone. They called you, made you come in, and sat you in a room while a resident who didn't look old enough to shave told you that your child was gone. "Why?" Gloria had asked the doctor, who had responded with something about a broken neck, killed instantly. But that wasn't what she was asking.

The whys continued. Why Amber? Why their family? Why had God done this to her? To *her*, as if Brian had not been party to it.

Brian didn't have anyone to ask why to. He knew there was

no rhyme or reason to it. Why them? Why *not* them? Why anyone?

"Why?" Gloria asked again after he hit the man in their bereavement group. There was blood splatter on the front of her pink blouse, the color so complementary it would've been pretty, had it not been born of such violence.

"Why, Brian? Why?" she demanded after Father Mercer accompanied the man and his wife to the hospital.

"Why?" Brian gritted his teeth. Did he really have to explain himself? After all this time? "Amber's death was God's will? God wanted her to die? What kind of asshole says that to a parent?"

"I've said it to a parent," she said. "So my kind of asshole, I guess." Gloria's mouth puckered, the curse word a strange fruit she had tasted and did not care for. "It's to bring solace."

"It's a bullshit platitude."

"Maybe from some people, but that man you punched—he's also a grieving parent."

Yes, Brian was aware. After years of his wife's harping, he'd finally relented and gone to the grief support group at the church, not that it seemed to be doing Gloria much good. But things were so bad between them, so brittle, he had agreed. And then he'd gone and it had been that same old crap. God's will. Brian was glad he didn't believe in God because the way these people spoke about him, he was a sadistic SOB.

"You're the one who wanted me to go to the bereavement group," Brian accused her, jabbing an angry finger in her face.

"Stop trying to force that religious crap down my throat."

"Forcing? I just wanted us to be around other grieving parents."

"That guy's kid died of cancer. It's not the same."

"How is it not the same?"

"His own body killed him. Someone killed Amber."

"Oh, not that again."

"Someone has to pay," Brian said. "You want me to have peace? Find the driver."

"That won't change a thing except give you someone to blame."

"Isn't that what you do? Blame it on God. Only you all don't say *blame*. You say *will*. But either way, you're pinning it on someone." Brian's face was red, the vein in his neck throbbing. "And anyway, I know who it was."

"Calvin?" Gloria shook her head. "You're being so irrational. The police cleared him."

"And the police have never made a mistake before?" he asked. "You trust that detective to do right by Amber?"

"Yes, Brian, I do."

"They had sex, you know?" Brian said. He'd never told Gloria that he'd found the condoms in Amber's room. He wanted to spare his wife that pain, that anger, so he bore it all on his own. But now he wanted to wound her. He wanted to draw blood.

"Good," Gloria said after a long silence. "I'm glad she got to experience physical love."

"And to think I thought your beliefs mattered to you!" He had never been this angry before, not at anyone, not even after Amber's death. But all this fury, trained on the woman he loved. He wasn't sure how they'd gotten here and he didn't know how they would get back. Or if they could.

"I used to think my beliefs mattered to me, too," she replied, and then she walked out of the church, leaving him there, alone.

AMBER

When Dad comes home that night, Mom sends Melissa and me to our rooms. We meet up in Melissa's.

"I feel like I'm ten years old, getting grounded for talking back," I say.

"Same," Melissa says.

"Since when did you ever talk back?"

"When I turned ten," Melissa says. "You missed the spicy stuff."

"A likely story. You were always the good girl. I don't even know how to die right." I pause. "I even ruined your birthday party."

"What birthday party?"

"Your spy party, remember?"

The party was notable because usually Missy didn't want to celebrate her birthday like that. Mom would always offer to

118

host friends or pay for a bunch of kids to go ice-skating or trampolining, all that regular stuff. But Missy declined, preferring a quiet family dinner with us and Aunt Pauline. But the year she was turning ten, she wanted to have an actual party. She spent ages working on assumed identities for all of us. She had plans to decorate each room differently. And then on the night of the party, we were going to spy on each other to try to figure out who was who. It made no sense to any of us except for Missy who'd worked out all the details.

The guest list was pretty much the same people—our family, Aunt Pauline, and also Calvin. When she showed me Calvin's hand-drawn invitation with his assigned character, I'd scoffed, "*This* is why you don't have any actual friends to come to your party." Thinking about it now, I'm disgusted with myself. Why was I such a bitch to her? Also, maybe it's the new perspective that comes with being dead for seven years, but a spy party sounds sort of cool.

"What day is it today?" I ask.

"April 28," Melissa says.

"You're turning seventeen soon!"

She smiles ruefully. "In a few days."

"Do you have exciting plans?"

"Not really," she says, but the pink dots in her cheeks tell another story, and I wonder if my sister has a boyfriend.

"Let me rephrase: Did you have exciting plans before I reappeared?"

Her cheeks are tomatoes now. "It's not a big deal."

"Turning seventeen is very much a big deal. And I should know, I've done it. I can't speak for eighteen, though."

Melissa rolls her eyes. "Death turned you into a comedian."

"I believe it's called gallows humor."

"You are living in a fantasy world!" Mom's voice booms through the house.

Melissa and I stop talking and put our ears to the door, though it's hardly necessary.

"No, I'm living in a miracle world," Dad shouts back, his voice equally loud but jubilant. "None of what mattered before matters now."

"It does, Brian. Life goes on for everyone else. Remember, we learned that after Amber passed and people got tired of dealing with us, dealing with you."

"Why are you stirring that up? That's all in the past. In a different life. Nothing that existed before applies. We're living in a post-miracle world."

"Will you listen to yourself!" Mom screams.

"Will you listen to yourself!" Dad shoots back.

Melissa opens her door. "If you shout any louder, everyone in the neighborhood will listen to you," she calls. "I'm not sure why you sent us to our rooms if you're going to scream."

Mom's sigh is so gusty you can practically feel it tunnel down the hall.

"Come on out, girls," Dad calls.

I look at Melissa, who nods, and I follow her, as if she were the older sister.

Dad opens his arms to hug us both. "There are my miracles."

120

He turns to Mom, who is sitting ramrod straight on a chair. "You used to call them that, Gloria."

"That was different. All children are miracles."

"I don't know. I've babysat some kids who were definitely borderline non-miracles," Melissa jokes.

"Did you really tell Father Mercer I'm back?" I ask Dad. Unlike Mom, I'm not upset. Maybe he's right and Father Mercer is the exact person to talk to. Even if he can't convince Mom I'm real or whatever, maybe he could help me understand. And then I could help Calvin see I'm back, that I'm not some demon, and this would make him whole again, which would make me whole again. We could get married like we always said we would. Father Mercer could officiate.

"No. He wouldn't have believed me," Dad replies. "But I told him a miracle of the ages has happened in our household and that he needs to come over to witness it for himself."

"When is he coming?" Melissa asks.

"Never!" Mom replies.

"He said he'd come by Sunday after church," Dad says.

"No!" Mom shouts. "You have to cancel."

"Now, *that* would look suspicious," Dad says.

"Then put him off. Tell him the miracle is that you believe in God now. If that is what's happening."

Dad beams at me. "I believe in Amber. How can I not?" He turns to Mom and in a softer voice asks: "How can *you* not?"

Mom jumps up from her chair and, shaking her head in dismay, says, "Go to hell."

Dad watches her leave and then turns back to us, his smile

121

a little brighter, a little faker than it was. "Don't worry, girls. She'll come around." To me he adds, "Your death was particularly hard on her." He says this as if he sailed through it, as if he didn't accuse my boyfriend of murdering me and then go crazy trying to prove his theory.

I've been waiting all afternoon to ask Dad about Calvin, but suddenly, it seems less important to rehash the past than to figure out the present. And present-tense Dad is happy. I want that for him. I want that for both him and Mom, for me and Calvin. So I let it go.

"I'm going to make upside-down dinner!" Dad announces. "Blueberry pancakes, bacon, home fries, the works." And with that, he bustles off to the kitchen.

I look back down the darkened corridor. Their bedroom, now Mom's bedroom, is at the end of the hall, the door shut, the Do Not Disturb sign hanging ominously. "Is there something we can do to help Mom?" I ask Melissa. "Like where's Aunt Pauline? Why isn't she here?"

"I think she's in New Zealand still."

"When is she coming back?" Aunt Pauline was always traveling, working for years as a flight attendant, and later, when she realized she wanted to be able to really see the places she flew to, quitting that job to temp for my dad's company. She'd work, save up, go off for a few months until she ran out of funds, come back, lather, rinse, repeat.

"She lives there now."

"Really?" No matter how far Pauline wandered, she always

promised to come back. She said we were her base. "But New Zealand's so far away!"

Melissa stares at her hands. "I think that's the point."

"What do you mean?"

"Mom and Pauline, they don't really speak anymore."

This is even more shocking than Mom and Dad's separation. Mom practically raised Pauline. They needed each other. Losing her would be like losing a child. And Mom had already lost one of those.

GLORIA

Eighteen Years Before

The day her little sister took her first trip as a freshly minted flight attendant, Gloria drove her to the airport. Amber came, too, strapped into her booster seat in the back of the car.

"I can't believe you're really leaving home," Gloria told Pauline.

"I'm twenty, a little old to be freeloading off my older sister, don't you think, Amber?" Pauline replied, turning toward her niece in the back seat.

"What's a freeloader?" Amber asked.

"It's a mooch," Pauline said.

"What's a mooch?" Amber asked.

"A twenty-year-old living with her big sister."

"Don't listen to her, Amber," Gloria said, turning to Pauline. "You know we don't feel that way. I love you. Brian loves you."

"And I love you most!" Amber called.

"You better, kid." Pauline turned back to Gloria. "But what was supposed to be a few months turned into years."

Growing up in their mother's house had not been easy for Gloria, but for Pauline it had been a nightmare. Gloria's stoic temperament was better suited to living with a woman as rigid and cold as their mother, whereas Pauline's more dramatic nature put her in perpetual conflict with the woman. When their father had been alive, he'd been a buffer, but after he died, their mother grew smaller, more scared, meaner. She and Pauline fought constantly until, four months before her high school graduation, Pauline was kicked out of the house. She had shown up on Brian and Gloria's doorstep in tears. Amber had jumped up and down in glee at the sight of her aunt's suitcase, and Gloria was feeling a version of the same. Amber had not necessarily been planned, but she was wanted. Still, priorities had to be reshuffled again to allow for the new child—Brian had given up on graduate school to start a business and Gloria became a stay-at-home mom until Amber went to school—all of which was wonderful and a blessing but also isolating and lonely.

The plan had been for Pauline to stay until the fall, but by the time graduation rolled around, she was happily ensconced in the spare bedroom of their house, helping out at Brian's company, and proving to be such a helpful third set of hands that Gloria was able to go back to school for her master's degree. So Pauline stayed for two years.

"I was glad to have you. I wouldn't have gotten my degree

without you," Gloria said. "And Amber loved having her auntie close."

"You should stay forever!" Amber declared.

"Nah," Pauline said. "Don't you want a baby brother or sister?" Amber nodded vigorously. "Well, you'll need my room."

Gloria hadn't told Pauline that she was pregnant, but could Pauline tell? Her sister had a sixth sense about these things. Still, Gloria didn't say anything. She wouldn't until twelve weeks. Though she believed it was God's will whether she had this child, better not to tempt fate.

At the airport, Gloria parked the car, and the three of them walked Pauline inside the terminal, all the way to the special security lane for flight crew.

"Wait!" Gloria said before Pauline went through.

"I have nothing but time," Pauline said with a grin. "You got us here two hours early."

"You can't be too careful," Gloria said.

"Beg to differ," Pauline replied.

"Here." Gloria presented Pauline with a small stickpin encrusted with three gems. She'd had it made special by the jeweler who had engraved their wedding rings. "This is allowed to go on your uniform. I checked with the airline."

"Of course you did," Pauline joked, smiling at Amber. She ran her finger along the stones. "I love it."

"It's pearl, turquoise, and peri . . . peri . . ." Amber stumbled.

"Peridot," Gloria finished. "That's your birthstone, your aunt's is pearl, and mine is turquoise."

126

"You might need to add an emerald in there," Pauline added with a wicked smile. "If I'm not wrong, that's the birthstone for Tauruses."

The doctor had put the due date at the end of April. Taurus territory. So Pauline did know.

Gloria pulled her sister in tight, remembering how she'd looked all swaddled up as a newborn. It had been a rough pregnancy for their mother, forty hours of labor and then an emergency C-section. After coming home from the hospital, she declared she needed time to heal and retreated to her bedroom, leaving ten-year-old Gloria to care for the baby girl. It had been summer vacation and those first weeks, as Gloria spent her days holding, feeding, burping, and singing to her sister, her heart had felt so full, almost too full, a sensation she would not experience again until Amber was born.

"Mama, me too," Amber called, and Gloria picked her up and she and her sister enveloped the child, who really they had both raised.

"I'm not gonna cry!" Pauline said. "It'll screw up my makeup." Nonetheless she wiped a tear from her lashes.

Gloria, who rarely cried, broke down.

"It's only five days," Pauline said. "And I'm still crashing with you until I find a place. You'll be sick of me in no time."

"Promise me you'll always come back," Gloria said.

"Promise me you'll always be here for me to come back to," Pauline said.

As they held each other and Amber, they promised.

AMBER

I know it sounds terrible, but Mom and Dad splitting up, I kind of get. Married couples divorce—50 percent of them, Casey used to tell me when she alternately wished and dreaded that her parents were going to join that statistic.

But sisters? Sisters like Mom and Pauline who were a mix of siblings and mother-daughter and best friends? How can they stand to be apart? They once communicated every day, even when Pauline was on the other side of the planet, emailing or chatting in the comments on the travel blog Pauline had set up so she could easily share pics of her trips with Mom and Mom could load pics of me and Missy.

When Pauline was in town, she was almost always at our house. Even after Gammy left Pauline her house—"So you don't end up homeless," she wrote in the will—she barely lived there, spending days with us and only going home to water the plants and sleep.

"How?" I ask Melissa.

"I don't know," Melissa replies. "I haven't seen her in years. She didn't come to your funeral."

I think back to the last time I saw Pauline. She was on her way to Mexico, but for a short trip because she was coming back for Missy's spy party. Why wouldn't she come back for the funeral?

"It makes no sense."

"I know," Melissa says. "I tried asking her what was wrong, but she just stopped communicating with me. Every time I talked to Mom about it, she got so upset. So out of some loyalty to Mom, I didn't push it."

"You don't see her when she comes home?"

"That's the thing. I stalked her online for a while, but I don't think she has come home since you died."

"What about her house?"

"Other people live in it now, so I guess she sold it or rents it," Melissa says. "But for a long time, it just sat there, empty."

I've been struggling to understand how Mom is now, but as soon as Melissa says this, I realize that like Pauline's house, she's there, and empty.

That night after everyone falls asleep, I sneak into Melissa's room and fire up her computer. I search for Pauline's blog, Glopal, a take on *global* and a mash-up of her and Mom's names.

It's still there but it's completely out of date. The last photos are seven years old, from that trip she took to Mexico. There's Pauline twirling in a street with brightly colored buildings—sunflower yellow, apple red. *It's like the girls colored the streets with their Cray-olas,* she had written. I scroll back. The trip before that was to Turkey. There's a picture of her on a beach with a little pigtailed girl. *On beach at Black Sea when I joined this little girl making sand-castles. Her name is Glorinha, Romanian for Gloria,* she wrote in the caption. *What do you think about that, sis?*

Mom had responded in the comments. *That you're too old to make sandcastles.*

Auntie Pauline had responded: *No one is too old to make sand-castles, Glo.*

This is how they were. Arguing, disagreeing, bantering, but always, always loving.

A message pops up on Melissa's screen. Thought you were turning in early but you're still up! You still haven't said what you want to do for your birthday. I am up for any-thing. xxLen

Len?

I remember my sister's pink cheeks when I asked her if she had birthday plans.

Len! So she does have a boyfriend! "You go, girl," I whisper at her sleeping figure. She snores softly, and in that moment I love her so much, it hollows out my belly. This was how Mom and Pauline loved each other.

It has to be because of me. Whatever went wrong between them. It's because of me.

Suddenly, coming back from the dead doesn't seem like a miracle so much as a curse. Because dead people don't have to see how much destruction they left in their wake. And me, I've got quite a body count going.

I ruined Mom and Dad's marriage. I ruined Mom and Pauline. I ruined Calvin. I even ruined Missy's tenth birthday.

Dad called my coming back a miracle, but how can it be? Mom was right. I'm not special. I never was. I didn't save orphans. I didn't march for causes. I didn't even pick up litter. And I was horrible to my amazing sister.

I was selfish. In life, and in after life. All I've been able to think about is me, what I've missed, getting my life back to how it was. But lives can end, even without the benefit of death. Just look at them. Look at all of them.

"I have to fix this," I whisper into the quiet room.

Melissa rolls over in her bed, making unintelligible sleep noises.

"I have to fix this," I repeat, an idea forming.

I can't go back in time and undo my death, but maybe I can undo the damage it wrought, starting with Melissa's birthday party. I go back to Aunt Pauline's blog.

"Auntie P," I write in the comments. "It's Missy here, now Melissa. I know it's been way too long but I'm having a party on my seventeenth birthday—think of it as a do-over for the spy party I never had. It would mean the world to me and Mom if you could come."

The original guest list was supposed to be Missy, Mom, Dad, Pauline, Calvin, and me. This time, it's going to be the same. Plus this boy Len.

I haven't heard from Dina, so if I want to reach Calvin, I have to take matters into my own hands. I switch over to the social media program that Melissa uses and pull up Casey's page and send her a message, once again as Melissa. This is Melissa, Amber's sister. Can you tell me how to get in touch with Calvin? I write.

And then, finally, I click on the message from Len. Birthday party in the works at my place. Stay tuned for details.

"Turning seventeen *is* a big deal," I whisper to Melissa, and then I tiptoe back into my room.

MELISSA

One Year Before

"When did you know?" Lenny asked Melissa. They'd just shared their first kiss in the break room of the thrift store where they both worked. It was after hours, the place quiet save for the pounding of Melissa's heart.

"On your first day here," Melissa replied, relishing the waxy feel of Lenny's lipstick on her own lips, the tangle of Lenny's neatly manicured nails playing in her messy hair. She shifted herself and rested her head in Lenny's lap, smiling as she thought of the day, one month—and an entire lifetime—ago, when Lenny had walked into the store to apply for the job working the cash register and arranging the displays.

Tristan, the store's manager, had offered the job to Melissa first but she'd turned it down. Most people didn't like sorting the used clothes that came in but she loved it, no matter how old, how stained, how smelly the items were. When she held a piece, she could sense the life of the person who had owned it. A pair of ripped jeans, with *I Heart Rob* markered on them—she imagined someone her age who'd had their heart broken by a boy named Rob, and, realizing he was unworthy, had gotten rid of the jeans. A smock with snaps up the back—she pictured a grandmother, pockets full of treats for her grandkids. A pocket watch—she imagined it being passed from generation to generation, the last of the line dying out, and now the watch was in search of a new family. A lot of people might consider these things junk, but Melissa knew they left a shadow presence behind. It was a way someone could be here and gone at the same time.

When Tristan introduced Melissa to Lenny, she felt a wave of energy travel from her head to her toes, stopping, for good measure, between her legs. Was this the proverbial lightning bolt? She'd never felt anything like it before. She'd had crushes, plenty of crushes, but nothing like this.

It wasn't just that Lenny was gorgeous—black bobbed hair, olive skin, Cupid-bow lips painted her signature red—and stylish, coming to work each day in the most incredible outfits: a 1940s rayon dress and combat boots one day, a skinny suit and ballet flats the next. That was window dressing. Lenny was forceful and funny and sharp. She could do the Saturday *New York Times* crossword puzzle. She loved cat memes. She had the best laugh, a low husky chortle with a snort at the end that made Melissa laugh every time she heard it.

And Lenny, she laughed all the time. Melissa didn't realize

how much she'd missed laughter in the years since Amber died until she heard Lenny's constant and boisterous chuckle.

"My first day here? Didn't know you believed in love at first sight." Lenny rolled her eyes—impeccably made up with charcoal eyeliner. "Anyhow, love at first sight is a narrative construct, like money."

"Bet you twenty dollars Tristan disagrees with you."

"Har, har, I see what you did there," Lenny said, kissing her neck. "And that's not what I was asking. I was asking when you knew you were gay."

Melissa closed her eyes; the fluttering in her chest was warm and light and golden, like happiness incarnate. She considered Lenny's question. "I think I always knew. I just didn't know what I knew. That's why I was always watching people. To see if they could help me understand myself."

"Baby spy. You must've been so cute." Lenny stroked Melissa's forehead and the pleasure was almost unbearable. She truly had not known a body, let alone *her* body, could feel this way. "Did watching other people help?"

"I think so. We have a neighbor who's a lesbian, and I don't know, I think when I met her, I recognized something in her. She helped me come out to my parents, but it was my sister who really got me through."

"How?"

"She was like two people. There was Amber as I knew her: drama queen, devoted to her boyfriend, always with her clique of girlfriends."

"A basic bitch?" Lenny says.

"Pretty much. But then there was this other side of her, so protective of me. So loving. I thought if she could be two people, so could I. I thought there was some secret."

"Was there?"

She smiles. "The secret was to be me. She told me that."

"So you came out when you were ten?" Lenny asked.

"Fourteen."

"I thought your sister died when you were ten."

At first, Melissa and Lenny circled each other, always finding excuses to be near the other. Lenny would join Melissa while she sorted the clothes, claiming right of first refusal on any potential thrift score. Melissa kept going to the cash register, asking Lenny to change a twenty for no reason except to be near her. Soon, they found themselves lingering after closing, leaving at the same time, walking in the vague direction of one of their houses, stopping for a frozen yogurt or a cookie along the way. They talked about silly stuff: Lenny's obsession with 1980s soap operas like *Falcon Crest*, Melissa's aversion to eating any foods that were red. And more substantial things. Melissa knew Lenny had done her DNA testing and had been surprised to find out she was 20 percent West African and had been trying to untangle that complicated heritage. Lenny, meanwhile, knew that Melissa was thinking of delaying college a few years; she wanted to travel, maybe follow in her aunt's footsteps and become a flight attendant. "A butch flight attendant," Lenny joked. "All the queers will be banging on their call buttons."

And of course Lenny knew that Melissa's sister had died.

But what Lenny didn't know was how constantly the sisters spoke. Daily. Much more than when Amber was alive and always out at play rehearsal, or hanging with Casey and Alexa, or being all couply with Calvin.

It had started before the funeral, when a thought would enter Missy's mind, a question, a musing, and Amber would be there, clear as can be, to reply to it. Even then, Melissa understood it wasn't really Amber. It was the part of Amber that lived in her. But it didn't seem to make a difference. Amber was there, Melissa could talk to her, and Amber would talk back. And this Amber was the best version of herself, the kind and generous and funny big sister.

Not long after her thirteenth birthday, when Melissa finally began to connect the words *gay, lesbian,* and *queer* to the mystery about herself she had long been trying to solve, it was Amber she told first.

I'm not like you, she said.

No shit, her sister had replied.

No, I'm really not like you, she had reiterated.

Thank God for that, the Amber in her head had returned.

Melissa didn't mind Amber being like this. On the contrary, it was how she knew that in some sense she really was talking to her sister. If Amber had said, *Oh, Missy, you're just like me,* Melissa would've known then she was some wish-fulfillment, Hallmark-card figment of her imagination. But this Amber, she sounded like Amber.

Melissa danced around telling her sister that she was gay until finally, one day, after Melissa said something vague about not being like everyone else, Amber had impatiently said, *Oh, just spit it out already.*

Melissa had not spat it out. She was not ready. But she was getting closer.

Several months later, she came out, really came out, to Amber.

I'm gay, she told her.

Actually, Amber replied, *you're kind of mopey. You're not gay at all. You could use more gaiety in your life.*

No, I'm gay, like I like girls.

But do girls like you back? It was such an Amber answer, so bratty and so comforting.

She came out to Amber every single day for months, to the point that Amber grew tired of it. *If a tree falls in the forest and nobody hears it, does it make a sound?* Amber asked.

What's that mean?

Amber rolled her eyes, exasperated. *Does it matter if you're gay if no one knows it? Particularly other girls who might also be gay?*

Melissa knew she was right. She knew she had to tell someone else, someone here, and she had an idea of who to confide in. She'd psyched herself up to do it when, once again, life got in the way and it had to be postponed.

Why aren't you telling anyone? Amber kept asking her.

She didn't tell Amber why. Only that she would.

And when she finally did tell Peg Weston, Peg held her hand

until she was ready to tell her father, who just seemed uncomfortable about the whole thing, and later Peg sat outside on the front porch when she told her mother.

"Do you really want to know about this?" Melissa asked Lenny, who was running her nails, lightly, across the lids of Melissa's closed eyes, amping up the agonizing pleasure flooding Melissa's body to an even higher pitch.

"I want to know everything about you," Lenny said.

"You'll think I'm weird."

"That's been established. You won't eat apples."

"I'll eat the yellow and green ones."

"The prosecution rests."

And so Melissa took a deep breath and told Lenny something she had not told anyone else, not her mother or father or Peg or Father Mercer or anyone at the teen support group she'd been sent to after Amber died, where she understood that she wasn't grieving like everyone else because she hadn't lost Amber the way everyone else had lost their person.

As she spoke, Lenny's hand stilled, falling to her sides, leaving Melissa's skin cold and questioning: Had she gone too far?

"What are you thinking?" Melissa asked after a nerve-racking silence.

"I'm wondering what I did right in this world to land a job at the same thrift store as you."

Hope flared in Melissa's chest. She'd been honest with Amber, and it hadn't hurt her. And then Peg. And her parents. And now Lenny. Life had beckoned her out of the shadows, and the sun felt so good on her face. She took another breath. "Good. Because I think I'm falling in love with you."

Lenny responded with a generous helping of her perfect laugh. "Oh, girl, I'm *already* in love with you."

"I thought love at first sight was a social construct," Melissa teased.

"Oh, shut up," Lenny said. And then, still laughing that musical, life-affirming, joyful trill of hers, she kissed Melissa, and after that, the talking stopped.

AMBER

When I get back to my room, Dina is sitting on my bed. "Jesus, you scared me!"

"Sorry," she says. And then she sneezes.

"Bless you."

"Thank you." She sneezes again.

"Are you sick?"

She shakes her head. "It's always allergy season for me, remember?"

How could I forget? Dina wasn't just allergic to food; she was allergic to dust, seasons, animals. She had to take a pill before she could come over or her eyes would go all puffy just at the sight of Mr. Fluff. On high-pollen-count days, she wasn't allowed to play outside at recess. In elementary school, I would stay with her in the library. I kind of loved those days when we had the books all to ourselves and were granted special dispensation to break the no-eating-in-the-stacks rule.

"I'm so glad you came back," I say. "I was scared you wouldn't."

"Why would you think that?"

Dina in ninth grade, eating at the lunch table designated for kids with allergies. Alone. Dina, sitting in the library. Alone.

But no, that was ages ago. And Dina had come to see me. She wouldn't be here if that still bothered her. I'm sure she's forgotten all about it. We aren't kids anymore, after all.

"Are you still grounded?" she asks me.

"For eternity, it would seem."

"Eternity is a long time," Dina says.

"Is it? Recent experience suggests otherwise."

"You're funny," she says. "You stopped being funny for a while."

"No, I didn't!"

"You kind of did. You were always worried what other people thought."

It's the kind of observation that should sting but doesn't. Maybe that's one of the benefits of maturity—if you can mature when you're dead. Also, it's hard not to recognize some truth in it.

"Yeah, maybe you're right. I was a kid." And it's funny because a few days ago, I still felt like teenage Amber, but now, it's like maybe I'm catching up to myself.

"I found Calvin," she says.

"You did?"

She nods. "I know where he lives. I can take you." She gestures to the window.

"What, like now?"

"Yeah, why not?"

I hesitate. "My parents don't want anyone to find out about me. They don't know I saw Calvin and I haven't told them that you've been coming over. I don't want to make trouble."

All this is true but it's not why I'm hedging. Five minutes after I messaged Casey, I got a bad feeling, the way I always used to when I did something impulsive. But it's too late now. I have to let it play out. And hopefully Casey will send Melissa Calvin's contact info and I'll invite him to the party, where he can see me with other people and believe it's me, and it'll be less fraught than before.

"Don't worry about me," Dina says. "I won't get in trouble."

"But I might, if someone sees us."

"No one will see us," she promises.

"Maybe we should wait," I say. "For Calvin to come to me."

"Suit yourself," she says. "I thought you wanted me to help you."

"I do. It's just . . ."

"What?"

I hesitate for a moment and then I tell Dina how earlier, I sent a message to Casey asking for Calvin's details.

Dina's brow furrows. "Contacting Casey Locke was a really foolish thing to do," she says in a quiet voice.

"I didn't do it as me. I was on Melissa's account. I'm not dumb."

"You don't think Casey will think it's odd that Melissa is reaching out after seven years?"

"Casey already thinks Melissa is weird." Though *weird* wasn't the word she used. *Loser* was what she said. *Pathetic. Embarrassment.* Casey always said it was a good thing that Melissa and I were so far apart in age because having her at the same school as me would damage my reputation. "I don't think Casey would put it together."

"Well, you knew her better than I ever did."

I get that bad feeling again. I did know Casey well. She was my best friend, but I never fully trusted her. I kept things from her, about me and Calvin, especially. But Dina I trust, even after all these years, even after what I did to her. And she wants to help me fix things.

I open the window. A warm blast of air rattles the shades. Dina sneezes. I climb through and turn back toward her. "C'mon," I say. "Time to get life back on track."

CASEY
Seven Years Before

Casey's mom was wearing a brand-new diamond ring. "Your father gave it to me," she said, holding her hand out to Casey. "Isn't he the sweetest?"

Casey nodded and faked a smile. Both she and her mother knew Casey's father was not even a little bit sweet. The diamond was a transaction. Her father slept around and paid for her mother's acceptance in carats.

It was a huge diamond. Maybe two carats. He must have gotten caught big-time.

If Casey ever got married—and that was a very big if—she was never going to be in her mom's position, which was to say the one with none of the chips. Her mom had been her father's secretary who'd given up her job once she snagged a husband. The woman was a walking, talking cliché of what not to do: a simpering wimp who swallowed his bad behavior so long as she had pretty baubles. No wonder her dad cheated. Given the choice, Casey would so much rather be the cheater than the cheated on.

Was this why she didn't feel guilty about Calvin? Even that first time, when she'd asked him to come over. It was the day after they'd all gone ice-skating, Amber and Alexa zooming ahead, leaving her and Calvin to trip their way across the ice together. Cal, I have an important question about Amber, she'd texted that next day. Need to discuss in person.

After she'd kissed him, had she felt guilty? Nope. She'd felt powerful, watching the blood rush to his face—and to parts farther south, judging by the bulge in his pants. He'd started to leave, turning toward the door before suddenly doubling back and pushing Casey against the wall, kissing her like he wanted to swallow her alive.

Looking at her mother's ring now, she did the requisite oohing and aahing before going upstairs. Come over, she texted Calvin.

"This is not happening again," Calvin had said as he'd buttoned his pants after that first time. "It's wrong." He said that every time now. They shouldn't be doing this. Amber was his girlfriend. Amber was Casey's best friend. Blah blah blah. Like she didn't know all that.

The thing was, she loved Amber, she really did. This wasn't about trying to hurt her. But Amber had so much, more than her fair share, so Casey felt justified in taking a piece, the way the government felt justified in collecting more taxes from rich people, something her father complained about all the time.

Twenty minutes later, Calvin was at her house. He parked his car down the block, just to be sure no one saw him, and texted before he got to the door. Casey left the front door unlocked, and her mother didn't notice Calvin enter over the blare of her TV.

They never spoke when he got there. He would walk in and they'd start kissing. And the kissing, well, Amber was always bragging about how tender Calvin was, so soft a touch for such a big guy. The way he kissed Casey wasn't tender at all. And that was fine. Casey didn't want it to be. It was usually over pretty quickly. After, he asked her if she wanted him to do anything to finish her off. So chivalrous! But she always declined. That wasn't the kind of satisfaction these after-school sessions gave her. So he'd go back into her bathroom to clean up, soap away their betrayal.

Today, after he went into the bathroom, Casey saw that his backpack had fallen off her desk chair, the contents spilling out. Casey didn't really consider it snooping. It was *her* room. And the papers were just sitting there. Upon closer inspection, she saw that it was actually a big four-color brochure from a college, emblazoned *Welcome*. Casey knew the school, a small private college, not the big state university that Amber said they were both attending.

Calvin came out of the bathroom and saw Casey crouched over his backpack. He looked at the papers, then at Casey. "Don't tell Amber."

At first Casey thought he meant don't tell her about them sleeping together, which she'd already assured him she had no desire, or reason, to do. But then he crammed the college brochure into his backpack and zipped it up with a violent tug.

Casey started to laugh. He wasn't just cheating on Amber with Casey. He was cheating on her with a college, too. Amber had been yapping about her "forever plan" with Calvin—same college, then marriage, graduate schools at different times—since the two had started dating. And now Calvin had applied to, and gotten in, somewhere else.

"Don't you think she's going to find out eventually?" Casey said when she'd regained control.

"Yeah, but not from you," he said. "This is between me and Amber."

"Sounds like it's *not* between you and Amber," she shot back.

"It's none of your fucking business, you hear me?"

She did not appreciate the tone of his voice. "You do not get to tell me what to do," Casey said. She had to work so hard to keep her own voice blasé. "I am Amber's best friend, and if I think there's pertinent information, then I'll—"

For as big as Calvin was, he was shockingly fast. In a single breath, he had taken her shoulders and shoved her against the wall. His face was close. She could smell the green-apple scent of her body wash, which he used to erase her, though if he wasn't such a moron, he'd know that the fruity smell of the soap was a much bigger giveaway.

She thought he might kiss her. She closed her eyes but nothing happened. She opened them and saw his eyes, curdled with disgust.

In spite of her reputation, Calvin was the first guy she'd slept with, but in that moment, Casey decided that whenever people asked her about it, she would lie and say she had lost her virginity with her high school sweetheart after a dance.

Calvin pushed away, snatched his backpack, and left her room. Dramatic as his departure was, Casey knew he'd be back.

And he was, the very next morning. He parked in her driveway without texting first and pounded on the door. For a brief second, Casey thought he'd come to profess his love. She maybe even hoped for it.

All that was dashed when she opened the door. The look on Calvin's face was pure hatred. Casey automatically stepped back into the foyer, shielding herself with the door, scared of what he might do to her.

"Did you tell her?" Calvin screamed.

"Did I tell who what?" she asked.

"Amber!" His voice cracked. "Did you tell her?"

Amber knew. A prickle of electricity lit through Casey, eating up the empty space where hope had just lived.

Calvin stepped inside and grabbed her by the shoulders. He yanked her back and forth, hard. "Did you tell her?"

Her father had not yet left for work and hearing the hubbub, he came to the front door and saw Calvin shaking Casey. "What the hell do you think you're doing?" her father shouted. She heard the anger in his voice and translated it as love. Another bolt of electricity shot up her spine.

"Get your hands off her!" her father yelled.

Casey could remember precisely one other occasion that her father had stuck up for her like this. Fifth grade. A softball game, Casey sliding into home plate as the umpire had called her out. Her father, who rarely came to games, had been there and made a scene. The umpire was an idiot. He was the father of a girl on the opposing team and biased. The umpire refused to amend the call and her father had taken her out for ice cream afterward as a consolation. The thing of it was, Casey *had* been out. She'd heard that thwap of the catcher's glove closing around the ball before she crossed home plate. But by the time her spoon scraped the last bit of hot fudge out of the silver bowl, she'd managed to convince herself that she *had* been safe.

"Get the hell out of here," her father yelled at Calvin. And when he still didn't move, her father punched him in the face.

The blow surprised Calvin more than it seemed to hurt him. He put his hand to his cheek as if unsure of what had happened. The skin under his eye was starting to swell.

As Calvin peeled out of their driveway, Casey started to cry. She looked to her father, expecting sympathy, but his face bore the same mask of disgust Calvin's had. "You lie down with dogs, don't be surprised when you get fleas," he told her.

It took her a minute to pull herself together so by the time she got to school, the first bell had rung, but there was a cluster of kids standing around the parking lot, crying. One of them was Alexa, who ran up to Casey and hugged her, crying, "Oh, Casey. I can't believe she's gone."

"Who's gone?" Casey asked.

AMBER

As if we agreed to it beforehand, once we are outside, Dina and I do not speak, do not break the meditative spell of the night. It feels safer this way. Like we stand a better chance of blending into the dark if we disappear into its hush.

We take my bike, me pedaling standing up while Dina sits on the seat, legs splayed into a V. We retrace the route I once took to school. Off our street, left onto Summit. I stop to look at the ghost bicycle I now know is a memorial to me. Dina touches it lightly as we pass, with a casualness that suggests habit. The streetlight flickers.

I pedal up the hill with ease, even with the added weight of Dina. She directs me to the left. I pause. Our town is laid out like a four-leaf clover. One leaf is the older developments where Dina and I live, one leaf is the mostly commercial area where Dad's office and the shopping mall are, one leaf is the newer developments, the fancier McMansions with spiral staircases and soaring foyers where Casey lives. The last leaf, the withering one, is the old industrial part of town, where the Whittaker Plant closed long ago. This part of town has several squat apartment blocks that once housed the factory workers, an area known as Whittaker Court but which everyone calls Witch's Coven.

Our town is not exactly a high-crime area, but whenever you read about a shooting or a drug bust in the newspaper, it was usually in Whittaker. The only people I knew who went there said they went to score drugs, which apparently was very easy to do, at least according to Casey. "You just drive up like at McDonald's," she'd bragged.

Though it was only a few miles from my house, I'd been to Whittaker only a few times, usually with our church, handing out Thanksgiving meals or warm coats. Even though it was broad daylight, even though I was surrounded by half our congregation, the place always felt shrouded in shadows.

Dina has me stop on an empty street. Wind blows trash and plastic bags across the way.

"There," Dina says, pointing to a window.

I follow her finger to a second-floor apartment. The window is bare, and a light is on, so Calvin is easily visible from the street. He's sitting at the table, staring off into space, occasionally taking a drink of something or other.

"Do you want to go in?" Dina asks me.

I do. I want to see Calvin. I want to fix things with him.

That's what I'm here to do. And I don't. Because seven years have passed and that man in that window is not someone I'm sure I know. If time has held still for me, it appears to have hurtled forward for him. He doesn't look twenty-five. He looks old.

"I can walk you to his front door but I can't go in with you," Dina says.

I'm sure Detective Weston has probably warned Dina against this neighborhood. She's probably breaking all kinds of rules even being here with me.

"Just give me a second to get my nerve up."

I hear myself. *Get my nerve up.* To see Calvin. My forever love.

He's standing up now, talking on a cell phone, and then he's put a coat on and then he's out of sight.

"Looks like he's going out," I say, relieved because this means I can't go in to see him.

"I think you're right." Dina points to the barred glass front door of the building. It opens and Calvin skulks onto the street, as if trying to diminish his height. As he walks under a streetlight, something hard and metallic glints in his hand. Is it his phone? Or a gun? The Calvin I know would never carry a gun. The Calvin I know would never hurt me. The Calvin I know would never work in a bar or live in Whittaker.

I duck behind a parked car, thinking of the article about Dad's crusade. My father who also loved me, who I also trusted, thought Calvin had hurt me.

"Does he have a gun?" I whisper to Dina.

She shrugs, her face impassive. Maybe being the daughter of a cop, she's spent her life around guns, though I remember when Detective Weston came home from work, before she even said hello, she would always put her firearm in a special safe.

"Let's get out of here," I say to Dina.

"Are you sure?" she says.

I used to be. So sure of Calvin. Of me. Of our future. But I was so young. Whatever I am, I'm not that anymore.

"I'm not sure of anything," I tell her.

CALVIN

Eight Years Before

The first time Calvin met Amber's parents, he brought flowers for her mother. His own mama had told him to. "Gotta win over the mother," she said.

"What about the father?" Calvin had asked, and she had tsked away the question, like fathers were irrelevant. Calvin's own father was. Irrelevant or absent. Same thing.

But it had been Mr. Crane who made Calvin's hands so sweaty with nerves that first night that he'd worried the silverware might slip right through his grasp. He must not have completely blown it because he was invited back, and the next dinner had been easier. After Mr. Crane made a passing reference to how his only regret about not having a son was having no one to toss a football with, Amber's sister had said, "I can catch a football," and so before the third dinner, Calvin had brought a ball with him. Mr. Crane and Missy had enjoyed

155

playing catch so much that on his fourth dinner, Calvin bought a nerf football—easier for Missy to catch, he thought—as a gift. By the fifth dinner, there'd been talk of a fly-fishing trip that summer while Amber was away at summer camp. Mr. Crane had even offered to loan Calvin a pair of his waders.

But then, that spring, abruptly, it all stopped. When Calvin came for the long-planned dinner the night before Amber left for camp, Mr. Crane declined to throw the football around. There was no mention of the fishing trip at that dinner, or during the following weeks. When Calvin emailed Mr. Crane to ask about dates so he could get his shifts covered, there was no response. All summer, as Calvin mowed lawns and whacked weeds and blew leaves and laid bricks, a sense of unease gnawed at his stomach, right next to the deep chasm of missing Amber.

"You're more whipped now than you were before you were getting some," Dean teased, reinstituting the meowing. This bothered Calvin. Not the pussy reference, which he was used to, but how right Dean was. How cleaved in half Calvin felt when Amber was away from him. How much he needed her to feel like himself. This kind of dependence was okay if they stayed together—and Amber insisted they would, first college, then marriage, and then happily ever after, just like her parents—but what if they didn't?

He had his first taste of what such a separation would feel like that summer. And he went full-on batshit, calculating days, then hours, then minutes until she came back. He requested extra shifts at work, to keep him busy and exhaust his body so his mind might click off at night and not obsess about Amber.

When Amber returned from camp, Calvin was not invited to pick her up from the bus, or to join the family for her welcome-home barbecue. He had to wait until the next day to see her.

She came over and they had reunion sex in his empty house. Afterward, when he was calmer, Amber's head cradled into the crook of his arm, he'd asked if her dad was okay.

"He's fine. Why?"

Calvin explained he'd been expecting them to go on that fishing trip together. "I guess he didn't go this year."

"Oh, he went," Amber said.

Calvin's heart had been lazy in his chest, anesthetized by the sex and having Amber in his arms, but now the engine of worry fired up again. "Did I do something to upset him?"

"Don't worry about it."

Calvin's heart pounded a hard two-punch, so powerful he was surprised Amber didn't feel it. "Don't worry about *what*?"

"Missy said he found my stash of rubbers."

Amber seemed to think this was amusing but Calvin felt sick to his stomach.

"Relax," she said. "I didn't get into trouble. He's just a little pissed that you stole my virginity. He'll get over it. I don't think he told my mom because I would've heard about that, and for the record, she wanted to invite you to the barbecue but Dad wanted it to be 'just family.'"

Calvin hated everything about this statement. Stole? Like he was a criminal. He'd been a virgin, too. It had been Amber's

157

idea to have sex. And "just family"? Amber *was* his family. But what he hated most was her laughing tone. How amused she seemed at the prospect of her father disliking Calvin. Maybe this was a luxury Amber could afford because she never had to worry about a father loving her. Not everyone was so lucky.

That was the moment Calvin understood how deeply intertwined he'd become with Amber. Dean would cite this as proof that he was whipped, but it was worse than that. It was like they were conjoined and now separation really could kill him. And in spite of Amber's happily-ever-after fantasies, separation now seemed possible. What if her dad forbade them from seeing each other? What if her mom gave her an ultimatum: Calvin or the family?

It was so fragile, what they had. It was a terrible feeling— this fear of losing something precious. Amber had backup: a big family, lots of friends. She'd be fine. But Calvin knew that he'd be useless without her. He *hated* that feeling, and for the tiniest flash, he hated Amber for causing it.

"Don't obsess over it," Amber said, kissing him in bed. "One day we'll be married and he'll have to love you, like my gammy had to love him, and then you can go on all the fishing trips you want."

They'd been talking casually about a future together like this for months now, but for the first time, Calvin didn't trust it. He could still see it happening, but now he didn't know if he wanted it to. Not if it could leave him this defenseless.

Amber looked at his bedside clock. "I have to go. I promised

Casey and Alexa I'd go ice-skating at the mall with them." She slipped out of bed, looking behind her. "Wanna come?"

The word *no* was on his lips. He wasn't a good skater and he tried not to invade Amber's time with her girlfriends. He didn't want to breed resentments, and anyway, while Alexa was cool, Casey had a sharpness that put him on edge.

But for whatever reason, that time, Calvin said, "Sure, I'll come."

AMBER

The next morning, while I'm pretending to sleep, the doorbell rings. I peek out my window and see that it's Detective Weston, and my first thought is that Dina got in trouble for sneaking me to Whittaker last night.

Mom answers the door. "Oh, Peggy," she says with a shudder in her voice.

Melissa opens my door, puts a finger to her lips, mouthing, "Be quiet," before heading toward the kitchen.

I hardly see the point in hiding. Mom already told Detective Weston about me and now she's here. But I don't want to risk getting Dina—or me—in any deeper trouble so I eavesdrop from the edge of the hall where I can hear them but they can't see me.

"Melissa," I hear Detective Weston say, her voice full of warmth.

"Hi, Peggy," I hear my sister say. There's the sound of kisses.

"Is Brian here?" Detective Weston asks. "I'd like to talk to all three of you."

Brian is not here. After their fight last night, Mom sent Dad back to his apartment. "You don't live here anymore," she'd said. Which had seemed even crueler than her telling him to go to hell.

"He's at his place." An edge has crept into Mom's voice. "But I can relay whatever message you have to him."

"Whatever you think is best."

"Let's sit down in the living room," Mom says, and they all move away and I can't hear them anymore.

I pad into the hall. I stop at the foyer, and when Detective Weston isn't looking, I dart across into the kitchen.

Melissa sees me and her eyes go wide, but she keeps her mouth shut. Her gaze goes to the end of the kitchen counter, where it L shapes into a cutting board. Underneath the board is a hollow space, one of Missy's favorite spy hiding niches. I nod as I hurriedly collapse my body into her hidey-hole.

"Thanks for being so supportive a few days ago," Mom is telling Detective Weston. "I think I had a brief lapse of sanity."

"It goes with the territory," Detective Weston replies.

"I'm just sorry to lay that on you."

Detective Weston reaches out to grab Mom's hand. "Gloria, you never have to apologize to me. For anything. We're family now." She reaches her other hand to Melissa.

Melissa told me that Mom and Detective Weston were

friends now and Dina confirmed it, but seeing it before my eyes, I can't quite believe it. The two of them had a chilly relationship from the start. Dina said it was because my mom was homophobic. I didn't even know what that meant at first, but I knew it was bad enough to tell Dina to shut up. Later I realized she was probably kind of right. Mom is, or was, a word-of-God kind of person and our church was not one of those that was super accepting of things like homosexuality.

But clearly all that is behind them now. Because Mom is acting with Detective Weston the way she once did with Pauline. Which is to say warm, vulnerable, letting her feelings show.

"So what brings you here, Peg?" Mom asks. "Not that you need a reason."

"No, but I do have a reason. I'm here, I suppose, on semi-official business."

I don't see Mom stiffen so much as feel it.

"What business is that?" Mom asks, trying to keep her voice steady.

"I got a call from the chief of police today."

"On a Saturday? Weren't you and Kathy going to visit her kids?"

"That'll keep. Anyhow, the chief had just come off the golf course with Scott Locke. Do you remember him?"

"Casey's father?" Mom asks. "Of course I do. I haven't seen him in years. What about him?" I can hear the effort Mom is making to sound casual. It's not really working, though. Her voice is brittle with fear.

"He wants us to open an investigation about those funds that were raised following Amber's death."

"Why?" Melissa asks.

"I have no idea," Detective Weston asks. "Normally, I'd write this kind of thing off, but with it coming on the heels of your voicemail message, I just wanted to check in."

The room goes sickeningly still. Mom buries her face in her hands and after a painful moment, looks up. "I think you know what happened to those funds. Brian spent them on detectives and billboards and his wild goose chase for a villain."

"No, you misunderstand me, Gloria. No one is asking you to justify how the money was spent," Detective Weston says. "You didn't solicit it. It was raised on your behalf. There were no stipulations given on how it should be spent. If you'd wanted to buy two thousand teddy bears, it would've been your right."

"So what you're saying is that Scott Locke is an asshole," Melissa says. "Not exactly breaking news."

"Language!" Mom's voice is so weak there's no muscle to her scold.

"I think my language is very precise," Melissa replies. "That whole family is awful. Casey was always such a manipulative bitch and she brought out the worst in Amber," she says, her voice louder, I expect, for my benefit. "Not that I can blame her, coming from those parents. Her dad screws everything in town. And her mom is even worse. So holier-than-thou. Remember how she complained to Father Mercer after I came out that I was bringing 'gay propaganda' to the church? Dude, it was a rainbow pin."

"I keep telling you to come to my church," Detective Weston says. "The Unitarians are very queer-friendly."

"I like my church," Melissa says. "I grew up in it. I can change minds from the inside. Like this one." She nudges Mom, who offers a wan smile and puts a hand against Melissa's cheek.

Two things strike me: One, Detective Weston doesn't know I'm back. And two, my sister is gay.

The first one is a surprise. Because if Mom didn't tell Detective Weston about me, then who told Dina?

But Melissa being gay? That feels like something I already knew.

"I'll refrain from commenting on Scott Locke while I'm here in a professional capacity, but now, let me change hats and talk to you as your friend." Detective Weston mimes taking something off her head and putting something else on it. "Gloria . . . Is there something you want to tell me?"

"No!" Mom's voice is a high-pitched squeak.

"Mom was having a moment the other night," Melissa says. "It just snuck up on her after all this time."

"I understand," Detective Weston says. "No matter how much time passes, I still can't believe it."

Mom turns toward the kitchen, unknowingly looking right at me when she answers. "I can't believe it, either."

PEG

Two Years Before

When Missy Crane knocked on the door, Peg was pleasantly surprised to see the girl, now more of a young woman. Though they lived on the same block, Peg had not seen her since the funeral.

"Hi, Detective Weston."

"I thought we agreed you'd call me Peg," she said, recalling their first meeting—what was it, more than ten years ago?

"Peg," she said weakly. "Can I come in?" She asked it so seriously, as if formally requesting an official appointment.

"Of course." She ushered her inside. "Would you like some tea?"

"I don't want to put you out," Missy replied.

"I always make tea this time of day if I'm home." She was not just saying that. Rituals helped punctuate her otherwise empty days.

"Okay," Missy replied.

Peg went into the kitchen to turn on the kettle. Missy followed behind her, solemnly watching.

"The honey is in the cabinet," Peg said, and Missy automatically went to the right one, as if she'd been here many times before. "Lemons in the . . ." But the girl had already retrieved one from the Delft china bowl that had come with the house.

Peg unearthed some unopened shortbread cookies from the cabinet—the sweet tooth that had hounded her, and her hips, her entire life had vanished—then set up a tray. She carried it back to the living room. Though it was a frigidly cold day, bright rays of sun warmed patches on the couch where they sat, side by side.

As they drank their tea, they chatted. Peg asked Missy about school and Missy asked Peg about her job on the force. To be honest, she was considering retiring, though she hadn't told anyone that. Nor had she said that part of the reason she wanted to leave was Amber Crane. Peg had only been tangentially involved in the investigation because no one really believed it was a homicide, but it weighed heavily on her that they had never found the driver. Mostly because she knew how much it weighed on the Cranes.

On the one-year anniversary of Amber's death, the local newspaper ran an update on the case. Peg had given a quote, referring to the low clearance rate for hit-and-runs. "Unfortunately, it's unlikely we will find the culprit, but at this point, I think it's more valuable to focus on the example of Amber's life rather than the tragedy of her death." A bit of generous poppy-cock, Peg thought, because though she had forgiven Amber, she didn't particularly consider her a beacon.

A few weeks after the article ran, she received an angry screed of an email from Brian, accusing her of not pursuing Amber's case because of some old enmity between the girls. The suggestion was preposterous. As if any of their juvenile squabbling mattered now. And even if it had, her professional standards wouldn't allow her to flub a case because of personal resentments. If she couldn't have investigated the case fairly, she would have recused herself. And the truth of it was, there was no homicide. It was vehicular manslaughter, not her domain.

A few months later, Earl Simcox, a retired cop who now worked as a private investigator, asked her out for a beer.

"What do you know about Calvin Judd?"

She sighed. "You're barking up a dead tree," she had told Earl. "We looked into him as a potential suspect for about five seconds because he had a black eye and didn't go to the funeral. The latter might be unorthodox but it's not unheard of. As for the black eye, it corroborated his rock-solid alibi. He was nowhere near the scene of the accident."

"Well, he's got quite the rap sheet now." Earl flipped open his notebook.

"That all came after," Peg said. "Grief makes monsters out of people."

Back then it had been a throwaway comment. Oh, did she know that now.

She looked at Missy as she sipped her tea and told the girl the truth. "I'm thinking of retiring."

"Why?"

"I suppose I don't feel like I'm helping people anymore. And really I moved here for Dina and she's not here anymore."

"I understand why you might feel that way but it's too bad."

"Why is it too bad?" Peg really wanted to know. She wanted this girl to tell her.

Missy drained the rest of her tea. Peg went to refill the cup, but Missy shook her head. She had seemed determined before; now she looked defeated.

"It's too bad," the girl said, "because *I* was going to ask for your help."

"You need my help?"

Missy's chin trembled. Peg remembered the first time they'd met. That ache in her heart. Here it was again.

"Tell me how I can help you, Missy."

The girl looked at her feet. "I'm gay," she said.

"Okay," Peg said, treading carefully, knowing how religious the mother was. "First of all, you should know that it's who you are and it's absolutely nothing to be ashamed of."

"I know," she said. "Amber told me that." She paused as if to correct herself. "Or she would've."

"She would have been absolutely right," Peg said. She would never forget what Amber had done to Dina, but if she had been at all accepting of her sister, it made Peg feel a little warmer toward the girl.

"I need to tell my family," Missy said. "I know it's going to hurt them and they've been through so much already." She looked up at Peg with watery eyes. "Will you help me?"

The Crane family had caused Peg Weston such a load of grief. First, Gloria rebuffed her. Then, Amber dumped Dina in the cruelest of ways. And following Amber's death, Brian came at her. Gloria had made some half-hearted attempts to be kind in the aftermath of everything. Too little too late, as far as Peg was concerned.

But she'd always felt a bond with Missy, a cord connecting them all this time. "I'll help you," she promised. "Of course I'll help you."

AMBER

Not long after Detective Weston leaves, Dad's truck skids into the driveway. This time, no one bothers to send Melissa and me away.

"What did she say?" Dad asks after Mom lets him in.

"She said Scott Locke was poking around, inquiring about opening an investigation into the memorial fund."

"Shit!" Dad says. "He emailed me last night."

"Why?" Mom's panic bounces off the walls.

"He asked about the fund. He wanted to see records of money spent."

Mom puts her hands to her throat. "Why didn't you tell me?"

"I knew it would only upset you. And anyway, as I wrote to him, I'm under no obligation to disclose anything to him."

"That's what Peggy said," Melissa adds.

Dad whistles, which is something he does when he's nervous.

"There's something else." He pulls out his phone and plays a voicemail message. "This is Nick Flores. I'm not sure if you remember me. I did that story several years ago that included your daughter Amber. I'm going to be back in town in a few days and I was hoping to follow up on some things, maybe ask you some more questions. I'll try again when I get there. Take care, bye."

As he hangs up, Mom's legs buckle. I go to catch her but Dad gets there first. "It's already starting," she says.

Even Dad looks shaken. "Maybe it's a coincidence."

"Or maybe Scott Locke called a journalist," Mom says.

"Why would he do that?" Dad asks. "I understand that me going to church or reaching out to Father Mercer is perhaps unusual, but it's hardly newsworthy, and anyhow, how would Scott even know?"

"Father Mercer might've told him," Mom says. "That family gives a lot of money to the church."

"But I didn't tell Father Mercer anything specific. Just that a miracle happened. I knew he wouldn't believe—couldn't believe—until he saw it with his own two eyes." Dad slumps into the old easy chair, putting his head in his hands. "I'm sorry, Gloria. I should not have made such a momentous decision unilaterally. I was just so overjoyed. I didn't think it through."

"It wasn't you," I say in a quiet voice.

"What wasn't me?"

"I mean that maybe it wasn't Father Mercer who tipped off Scott Locke or the reporter. It was maybe me."

"You?" Mom asks. "How?"

"I kind of messaged Casey from Melissa's account. Looking for Calvin."

"Amber!" Melissa exclaims. It's the most upset I've seen her.

"Why on earth would you do that?" Mom snaps. She's already mad. And I haven't even told her the next part.

"I did that because when I went to see Calvin, he freaked out."

"You went to see Calvin?" Mom roars, and then she and Dad are both shouting at once in concert about what a terrible, terrible idea that was. After they've finished their duet of disappointment, Dad turns to Melissa.

"Did you know about this?" he accuses.

Melissa braids her fingers together, nods.

"Why didn't you tell us?" Mom demands.

"Amber asked me not to. And I didn't think she'd reach out to Casey."

"I was trying to get in touch with Calvin so I could invite him to your birthday." I turn toward Melissa. "I wanted to fix the party I wrecked."

"What party?"

"The spy party you were supposed to have for your tenth birthday. Where we were all going to have secret identities and had to figure out who was who. I was so shitty to you about it. So mean. And then I ruined it."

"You didn't ruin my party!" Melissa says.

"I did. I've ruined so many things." I look at Mom and Dad. I think of Calvin and his possible gun. Of Pauline. I ruined them with my death. "I thought if I could fix things with Calvin and with your party then maybe me coming back would make sense. Maybe I'd start to feel more . . . normal. Maybe Mom and Dad would get back together." I turn to Mom. "Maybe then you could love me again."

Mom stands there for a moment, her face closed off like a statue. And then a tear leaks out. Followed by another and another until the tears are a torrent waterfalling down her face. "I have never stopped loving you," Mom says in a shuddery voice. "Not for one single second. Sometimes I wish I could. Maybe it would hurt less. But as long as I draw breath, I will love you."

"Then why are you so mad that I'm back?" I cry.

"Because I'm terrified to believe it's you. Because how can it be you even if it seems to be you and if it's not you—and it can't be you, can it?—then I'll have to lose you all over again. And I don't know if I could survive that. I barely survived losing you once."

And then the dam bursts and Mom is sobbing and instead of waiting for her to embrace me, I go to her. Mom lets me hug her and then she pushes me away and for a second I think she's going to reject me again but she doesn't. She just inspects me, and though I have no memory of being born, I have the sense she looked at me this way then, too, like she was meeting someone she already knew.

After a moment, she yanks me toward her, squeezing me. I can't say that I feel it, really feel it, but the cold that's set in my bones since I got back lifts. I feel, if not the warmth of her body, the warmth of her love. And then Dad is hugging Mom and Melissa is hugging me and we are all hugging each other.

"What are we going to do?" I ask.

"I don't know," Mom says. She's drying her eyes and zipping up her resolve. I can see her vertebrae stacking, growing taller, stronger. "But we will figure it out. Together. We will figure it out as a family."

CASEY
One Day Before

Casey was getting dressed for a late-night hookup with the latest swipe-right guy when her phone rang. Usually the only person who called her at this hour was her mom, slurring drunk, complaining about her father's latest affair. It had gotten to the point where Casey stopped answering.

But the name that flashed on her screen shocked her. It was one she hadn't seen in a long time.

"Yes," she replied, drawing out the hiss of the word to buy herself time, to calm her pounding heart.

"It's Calvin," he said, adding, "Judd," as if there were so many Calvins in her life.

"Calvin, long time," she said. The singsong in her voice tasted artificial, like the kind of fake sugar that left an aftertaste and gave you cancer. "What's up?"

They had not spoken in person since the morning after

Amber died, when he'd indirectly accused Casey of somehow being at fault, as if Amber finding out about Calvin would send her purposely careening into a moving car. The girl was ridiculous and swoony about Calvin, but she wasn't that stupid. And anyway, Amber was from a churchy family, who would think suicide was a sin. The whole accusation was so insulting that when Casey first learned Mr. Crane had gone all commando trying to pin Amber's death on Calvin, it felt like some sort of cosmic justice.

Calvin didn't answer her, making Casey do all the work, just like when they were teenagers. "I'm on my way out, so if this is a catchup—"

"Have you seen Amber?" he interrupted.

Before the rational part of Casey's brain could process the absurdity of the question, a different part, the sixteen-year-old-girl, heard it. The sting of it returned. Amber. It had always been about Amber.

"Have I seen Amber?" she repeated, firing each word like bullets in a chamber.

"I know it sounds strange."

"It doesn't sound strange," Casey replied. "It sounds *insane.*"

Insane was how Casey's father had described Calvin to the police when he'd been questioned about punching Calvin the morning after Amber's death. "I wouldn't put it past him to kill someone," he'd said.

Except he hadn't, of course. Calvin had an alibi. Casey was the alibi.

"No, Officer, he did not knock his girlfriend off her bike, because at the precise time of Amber's death, Calvin was screwing her best friend." That wasn't exactly how Casey had put it, but the gist of it was the same. The detective's lip had quivered as she'd written it down on her little pad, the disgust emanating off her like radiation. Fuck her. Fuck Calvin. Fuck them all. But at least the detective had kept it quiet. Calvin was cleared and life went on and that might've been the end of it had Amber's dad not gone so completely bonkers, with stupid billboards and newspaper ads and private eyes until Calvin's mother very publicly spilled exactly where Calvin had been the day that Amber died. The Locke family's carefully cultivated reputation was trashed after that. Casey, the grieving best friend, became the boyfriend-stealing slut. It never seemed to occur to people that you could be both.

All this had happened during her junior year of college, when high school felt like ancient history, but that hadn't stopped all her friends at home from dropping her, or her own father from suggesting she not come home for the summer break. "Better to stay away until things settle down," he said.

Honestly, they'd all done her a favor. That podunk town was in her rearview mirror and she was never going back. And she hadn't. She'd graduated from college with a marketing degree, gotten a well-paying job at a pharmaceutical company, rented a high-rise apartment with a view of the city, and gone out to nice dinners with friends who had never heard the names Amber Crane or Calvin Judd. Aside from her parents—who she saw for their annual vacations to Europe—she had severed all links to her high school self, and honestly, if she could cut ties with her parents, she would.

"I know it sounds insane," Calvin said. "But I saw Amber."

"You saw Amber?"

"Twice. She came to the bar and I swear I just saw her out my window."

"Jesus, Calvin, isn't like the first rule of drug dealing not to sample the inventory?"

She didn't believe him, obviously. She was a rational human being. But that didn't mean that this didn't awaken something she had shoved in the far reaches of her mental closet. Seven years dead and he was still pining for her. Still wanted her.

"Have you heard from her?" he asked. "I can't go to her family. You're the only other person I could think of."

So she was a consolation prize, again. Sloppy seconds, even now. All the tendons in her neck tightened, like a spring about to snap. She took a deep breath, sharpened her knife, and in a quiet, almost reassuring voice, went in for the kill. "I have not seen Amber," Casey told Calvin. "Because she is dead and I think you should know that I did actually tell her about us. That afternoon just before she died. She ran off crying and rode her bike home and I texted you to come fuck me and you did."

None of it was true but in that moment, she wished it were.

She hung up the phone and blocked his number and erased him from her contacts. And for good measure, she purged every other contact from home. It felt so good, taking control like that. She should've done this years ago.

A text came in from the guy she was supposed to meet, asking Where are you? She blocked him, too, unliked him on the app. Unliked all the other guys she was half dating. None of them deserved her.

She moved over to the social media app she'd once spent hours a day on but had avoided after some of her so-called friends from high school dropped her. As if they were so perfect, as if their shit didn't stink. She searched for Alexa's profile. Alexa hadn't blocked her. She'd done something worse: sent her the most sanctimonious message saying that Casey had desecrated Amber's memory. Then she'd barely communicated with Casey, save for the occasional birthday wish, as if Casey was some charity case.

Unfollow. Casey stabbed at her keyboard, severing the relationship with Alexa once and for all. Fuck her and all those other self-righteous fair-weather friends. *Unfollow,* Casey pounded the button with relish. *Unfollow, unfollow, unfollow.* Why hadn't she done this years ago? It felt so good, like getting rid of clothes you didn't wear anymore. Clear out the closet to buy more stuff, better stuff.

And that was when she saw it. A message from Melissa Crane. She had not heard from Amber's weird little sister since the funeral. Nor had she expected to. Casey couldn't stand that kid, and she had sensed the feeling was mutual, which always pissed Casey off because that dork Missy wasn't cool enough to dislike Casey. But here she was, after seven years, reaching out to Casey, and asking about how to get in touch with Calvin.

A wave of nausea rose up in her so suddenly, she didn't have time to get to the bathroom and was forced to retch into a plastic shopping bag. Calvin calling asking about Amber. Melissa writing asking about Calvin. Her heart started to pound and black spots skated across her vision the way they had that day in the parking lot when Alexa told her Amber was dead. She was scared, and there was only one person she could think of who might make it better.

She picked up the phone. She called her father.

AMBER

Dad calls a family meeting.

Mom makes tea. Melissa pops popcorn. We all gather on the couch like this is any other discussion to talk about slacking off on chores or treating one another with more respect. It's like nothing has changed.

But everything has changed.

Dad clears his throat. "I cannot pretend to understand how it is you are here with us, Amber, but I have decided it's not for me to question." Dad looks at Mom with a familiar tenderness. "Your mother always said God works in mysterious ways. I should've trusted you."

"How could you when I couldn't trust myself?" Mom replies. "And none of that matters now. What matters is that we're here. Together. How that is, why that is, we may never understand."

"That's what makes it a miracle. Your mother always said

both of you girls were miracles. So maybe neither of us should be surprised that we've been bestowed with another one," Dad says, reaching for Mom's hand. This time she does not shake it off.

"We may never agree on how or why you are here but we agree on one very important thing," Mom says. "We have to protect Amber."

"How?" I ask.

"By leaving."

It makes sense. Whatever I am, I no longer fit into the mold of my old life. I have to go away, start life somewhere new, as someone new. My family could come visit me. Dina could come visit me. But no one else would ever have to know. I mean, maybe I'm not even the only one. Maybe there's a whole bunch of dead people who've come back on the down-low, like in some kind of witness-protection program.

"When do I go?" I ask. "Where do I go?"

"Not you," Mom replies. "Us."

"The whole family," Dad agrees.

"Where?" Melissa asks.

"As far away as possible," Mom says.

"Where no one knows us," Dad adds.

"But what about . . ." Melissa trails off. She takes several deep breaths, like she's trying to calm herself. But I think I know what she wants to say. *What about me? What about the girl I am in love with?*

"I know it will be hard with Lenny," Mom says. "But you're

182

about to graduate and start a new life anyhow."

"And you're young," Dad adds. "You'll meet someone else."

"How can you say that?" I cry. "You two met when you were only a few years older than Melissa is now. Maybe Lenny is the love of her life. I won't let you ruin it on my behalf." I turn to Melissa. "I won't let them do that to you! I'm sorry I wasn't a better big sister before, but I'm going to change that now." I turn back to Mom and Dad. "Send me away. Let Melissa have her life."

"How can I do that?" Mom asks. "Maybe it's selfish but I can't lose either one of you now. Melissa understands that."

Does she? My sister has folded herself into a ball, hands clasped around her knees, as if trying to make herself invisible, but I see her body quaking. I rush to her and encircle her in my arms, holding her tight as I can, refusing to let another thing break apart because of me. I thought I knew love before. I talked about it all the time with Calvin, but what I feel now for my sister is a tidal wave, taking over my entire body, a different kind of love than anything I've ever experienced. I wish I could've protected her better when she was younger. She claims I did after I died. And I'll be damned if that's going to stop because I came back.

"I refuse to let this happen," I tell Mom and Dad. "You can go back and forth between here and wherever you want to send me. You can take turns, like how divorced parents share custody."

"But then we'd have to be apart from each other," Dad says.

"And there's already been too much of that."

He looks at Mom, who nods at him, a tiny gesture, but it's enough. They are going to try again. It was one of the things I wanted, one of the rifts I needed to mend, but not like this. Not at Melissa's expense.

"'Someone has to die in order that the rest of us should value life more,'" Melissa says in a quiet voice.

"Huh?" I ask.

"The Virginia Woolf quote from your yearbook," she says between juddering breaths. "It means you have to lose something to value something else." She swipes her sleeve across her red-rimmed eyes. "And maybe it means I have to lose Lenny."

"No!" I cry. "That's not what it means!"

"I think it does," she says, her quaking subsiding, and like Mom before, I can see her posture change as she comes to peace with the decision. "It doesn't have to be forever. But it does have to be for now."

Dad kisses the top of her blue-haired head. "Thank you, Melissa."

Mom takes her hand. "We'll make it up to you. Anything you want."

And so it's decided. Without me. In spite of me. Because of me.

I don't deserve Melissa. I never did. But I will spend whatever days I have left living up to this sister of mine.

Melissa smiles through watery tears. "For a start, how about that dog you promised?"

ARNOLD
Five Years Before

During his third summer of driving Arnold King discovered the pet shelter. It was two towns over. How many times had he driven past the place, ignoring the sign out front exhorting him to "Paws for Love"?

He pulled his car into the driveway. Over the years, friends had recommended he get some sort of pet, assuming he needed to assuage his loneliness, but he never felt the urge. That wasn't why he stopped. He stopped because it was a new place and stopping was what he did now. When he opened the door and was walloped with a most acrid smell of wet fur and ammonia, he nearly turned around.

But before he could, a woman said, "Welcome." Not wanting to be rude, he walked into the shelter and shut the door behind him. The woman, about his age with a wild mass of curly silver hair, was holding a kitten in one hand and cleaning a litter box with the other. "Let me know if I can introduce you to anyone."

He'd been charmed by that. *Introduce you.*

The door opened again. In came a woman. She was familiar but so were many people around here, a byproduct of having taught one hundred-plus students a year for decades.

"Ah, you've come back for Barley," the older woman said.

"I have," the younger woman replied in a tremulous voice. "Thank you for all your patience, Nancy."

"Picking out a new family member is a process." She turned to Arnold and handed him the kitten. "Here, hold her for a second."

"But I . . ." Arnold began, but she was gone before he could tell her he was not much of an animal person. The kitten also didn't appear to get the memo, as she inserted herself into the crook of his wrist and began purring with a muscle-car motor.

The older woman, Nancy, returned with a small wiry-haired gray dog on a leash. When he saw Arnold, he barked and jumped on his hind legs. The cat in his arms looked up for a second and then promptly went back to her nap.

"No, Barley," Nancy said. "He's not your new human. *She* is. This is Gloria and she's going to take you home." She led the impish mutt toward Gloria, who crouched down to scratch him behind the ears. Then she began to cry.

Out of nowhere, Nancy produced a crisp blue handkerchief and gave it to the crying woman. "It's all right."

As Gloria dabbed her eyes, the dog wandered over to Arnold and wound its leash around his legs until he was immobilized, with a weeping woman to his right and a kitten in his arms. This was not a scenario he'd ever imagined himself in.

"I promised my daughter a dog," Gloria was saying, "and I couldn't handle a puppy but an older dog might . . ." At that, a fresh round of tears poured from her eyes. "It's just, I lost Mr. Fluff not long ago and you saw how hard that was on me."

"I did," Nancy said, putting her hand on Gloria's wrist. "It's okay."

"You must think I'm an idiot."

"Not at all! I know how painful it is to lose something so precious to you," Nancy said, her voice soft, her expression knowing.

"I just don't know if I can do it again. I don't know if I can handle that loss again." She directed this, for some reason, to Arnold.

Suddenly he recognized her, remembering her from parent-teacher conferences. And from the funeral.

"I understand," he said, even though how could he? One benefit of being single, childless, petless, was that you didn't open yourself up to that kind of loss.

"I feel so terrible," she cried. "What will happen to the dog if I don't take him? He won't go to the pound, will he?"

Arnold very nearly volunteered to adopt him but before he could, Nancy said, "Don't worry. Another family has already inquired about him so I think he'll get scooped right up." Arnold, who was not an animal person, nevertheless suffered a wave of disappointment.

After Gloria left, the air in the shelter seemed to have changed. Alone facing Nancy, holding the kitten, Arnold felt awkward, tongue-tied, and so very young.

"She took your handkerchief," he said.

"Oh, I keep a stack of them. Tears happen here more often than you would think." She gestured for Arnold to hand the kitten back. As soon as he did, the spot where she'd been nestling felt much colder.

"I would think adopting a pet is a happy occasion," he said.

"It often is, but sometimes it's bittersweet," Nancy said, depositing the kitten back into the cage, where she did three clockwise circles before lying down in a ball. "Some people adopt pets to fill the void of some other loss." She bent down to scratch Barley between his ears, while his tail beat a staccato rhythm against a shelf. "I started volunteering here for the same reason."

"Your husband?" Arnold asked perversely, hopeful that she was a widow.

"Oh, Tom died twenty years ago. My son, Jeremy. He didn't die. He disappeared. Which is harder."

"I can only imagine."

"Sorry, that's a lot to unload on you."

"I don't mind." And though Arnold had cultivated a life to avoid people unloading on him, this was true. He was happy for this woman to tell him anything she wanted to.

"So does this guy really have another family who wants him?" he asked.

"Oh, Barley. My old-man mutt sweetheart. He's been here a while. Not a lot of takers, but I've been wanting to bring him home, and I think this was just the push I needed. All was meant to be in the end."

Paws for Love. That's what the sign had said. Arnold generally disliked sentimentality as much as he did puns, and he certainly did not believe in anything like fate, but in that moment he had a vision of Nancy on a couch, reading a book, and him next to her grading papers. Barley on a pillow at their feet, the kitten, now a cat, they would name Lady, in his lap. He could see it so clearly—this life so different from the one he'd known. It was right there.

"Nancy," he said. "I hope this doesn't sound hasty, but I would like to adopt that kitten and I would like to take you to dinner."

The look on Nancy's face was one of pure shock, as if she had not expected the day to go that way. Then again, neither had he. But in the last three summers, he'd trusted the road to take him where he needed to go. And it had taken him here.

"I'll need you to fill out an application and provide references." She handed him a sheaf of paperwork. "And we're closing soon so you probably can't collect the kitten until tomorrow."

She'd sidestepped the dinner invitation. He wasn't surprised. A sixty-six-year-old bachelor. Not much of a catch. She didn't even know his name.

That vision, though—it had been so strong. He took out his marking pen and clicked it open. He would go through with the adoption, if not the dinner. He filled out the application, listed two references. Handed it back to her.

She peered at it. "Thank you, Arnold." She put the papers down. "As for dinner, I'll need to get Barley settled at home tonight, but why don't you let me cook you dinner tomorrow night after you collect the kitten. You can even bring her if you want. I have some old cat bowls and a litter box you can have. And she's quite fond of dogs."

The vision struck Arnold again. It would happen. It was already happening. He had paused for love. And love had paused back.

What a wondrous place this world could be.

AMBER

M om and Dad disappear into their bedroom and when they come out a while later, Mom announces the plan. We are moving overseas.

"Really?" I ask. "I was thinking we'd move across the country or something."

"We have to get far away. Possibly get new identities," Mom says. "Your passport, Amber, is thankfully still valid."

We got it just before graduation so I could take a trip to Tulum with Pauline. I remember how it was good for ten years.

"I think if we do a land border crossing they won't check," Mom says. "We get to Mexico and can fly from there and once we're somewhere new, we look into getting false identities."

"Mom, I never knew you had such a criminal mind," I say.

"Desperate times call for desperate measures," Mom says.

"Happy desperate," Dad clarifies. "Good desperate."

"What are we going to do for money?" Melissa asks. "Can we sell Dad's business? Or the house?"

"We can't do anything to arouse suspicion," Mom says. "We'll have to come up with some kind of public excuse why we're going away. We can say it's some sort of family emergency with Dad's family since he's not from here."

"We should make it public, so it doesn't seem like we're slinking off," Dad says.

"We could announce it at church," Mom says. "Tomorrow. Go as a family to say our goodbyes."

"And I'll clarify the miracle with Father Mercer," Dad says. "Say that my sister was cured of stage-four cancer or something."

"You don't have a sister," Melissa says.

"Father Mercer won't know and God won't mind a little fib to protect Amber."

"Maybe we say the miracle is that we're a family again," Mom says, looking at Dad, then Melissa, then me. "After what we've been through, it counts. And it wouldn't be a lie."

Dad puts his hand on hers. "No, it wouldn't," he says in a quiet voice.

"That still doesn't answer the question about money. How will we live?" I ask.

"For starters, there's still seventy thousand dollars left in the memorial fund," Dad says, looking to Mom.

She nods and adds: "And Pauline sold her house a few years back and left some of the proceeds to me. That's two hundred thousand right there."

Dad and Melissa both gasp out loud. This is news to them. "Why'd she do that?" Melissa asks.

"I don't know. I never used the money," Mom says. "So it's just sitting in an account, accruing interest. We'll use that. Then we can transfer the deed to this house to her and she can live in it or sell it." Mom pauses solemnly. "If she ever comes back."

Her face twists in pain, the way it would when she'd get one of her migraines. I'd assumed that Mom had estranged herself from Pauline, the way she had with Dad, the way she had with me, even when I came back. But now I see it's the other way around. Pauline cut off contact with Mom. How? Why? Aunt Pauline needed Mom. She always had. Mom was the only real mother she'd ever known, she'd told me over and over when I was little.

I sent her the invitation to Melissa's party assuming she'd *want* to come back, that she'd been waiting for an opening. It hadn't occurred to me that Mom was the one waiting for her own invitation.

She lost us both. Poor Mom. Poor Pauline.

"Why did Pauline go away?" I ask. "Why did she stop talking to you?"

"She thought it was her fault," Mom says. "Because she got you the bike. She said she couldn't face me. Couldn't face herself."

"That's ridiculous," I say.

"I know," Mom says quietly. "I should've tried harder, but honestly, when two people are drowning, they only drag each

193

other under. I couldn't save her. I couldn't even save myself."

"But now we can! We can move to New Zealand. We can all be together again."

"That's the first place they'd look for us," Dad says.

"*If* they look for us. Which they might but even so, who cares? This is Pauline!" I cry. "She's your sister." I look at Melissa now. I can't imagine ever being separated from her like that. It would kill me. Again.

"I know," Mom says softly. "And you're my daughter. And right now, being with you is my priority."

She takes my hand and squeezes. There are tears in her eyes, a smile on her face. For her, the sacrifice is worth it. Was Melissa right? Was Virginia Woolf right? You have to subtract something to add something? Gain a daughter, lose a sister. Gain a daughter, lose a life. Why is the common denominator losing? Why is the common denominator me?

NICK
One Day Before

The invitation had been emailed eight weeks before, but Nick had only opened it the previous week as he caught up on his backlog of messages in the Sydney Airbnb he'd rented in between assignments.

Arnold King and Nancy Halyard invite you to celebrate second chances . . .

It was a wedding invitation. "Good for you, Arnold," he said to his laptop screen.

When Nick had gotten his advance copy of the *National Geographic* article with the photo essay about ghost bicycle memorials, he'd sent it to Arnold, care of Kennedy High School, with a sticky note that said, *You were right!* Arnold had written him back, care of the magazine, and after that the two had kept up a steady correspondence, at first by airmail letters and then when Nick's globe-trotting and lack of a permanent mailing address made that impossible, by email.

Nick shared stories of the adventures from his photojournalism assignments, which had fallen from the skies like raindrops after the *National Geographic* article. Arnold updated Nick on his own life, more eventful than he could've imagined. He'd gotten a cat named Lady and a dog named Barley, and moved in with his girlfriend, Nancy, and recently retired from teaching. And now, here they were, getting married. Sitting on the veranda of his rented apartment overlooking Bondi Beach, Nick couldn't help but feel that it was Arnold's life that was exotic, enviable.

The wedding was in less than a week, but he had time between assignments and more airline miles than he could ever use. He could do it. He hadn't been back to that town—miserably working for Ansel Fitch Photo Studio, assuming his life was over at thirty-three—since the *National Geographic* piece launched his career, sending him all over the world. There was no reason to go back. He had no family there, no particular connection save for an old dead-end job, but suddenly he felt a pull to return. He would see Arnold again, the first time in person since they'd met near Amber Crane's bicycle memorial. And perhaps he would contact Amber's family. He'd contemplated this for years, wanting to tell them how their daughter had altered the trajectory of his life, but he'd held back, unsure if this would be comforting to them or reopen old wounds.

It was now well past the RSVP date but Nick emailed Arnold and Nancy that he would love to come. Arnold responded immediately. "Delighted! Will you be bringing anyone?"

There was no anyone, just a parade of someones. "It'll be just me," he wrote back.

Two days later, he sat in a bar at the Sydney airport, having second thoughts. His head was already fuzzy with jet lag, anticipating the sixteen-hour flight ahead of him, which was just the first leg before his connection. He sighed, loudly.

Next to him, a woman, said, "I second that emotion."

He turned to her. She was tall, sun-burnished, eyes crinkled with smile lines. "Sorry," she said. "I'm a nosy parker."

"So am I," Nick said. "By profession."

"Are you a spy?"

"Close. Photojournalist."

"I didn't realize they still had those." She gestured to her smartphone.

"It's a dying profession."

"Everything is, when you think about it."

Her accent was hard to pin down, softer than Australian, maybe Kiwi, with a twang underneath.

"Where are you from?"

"Take a guess." Her eyes sparkled with mirth.

"I'm gonna say Australia but that you've lived abroad a lot."

"Not sure whether to be flattered or insulted. From the States originally but I've been living outside Christchurch, New Zealand. Heading back for the first time in seven years."

"Seven years, how very biblical."

"You don't know the half of it," she said.

"And what's bringing you back?" Nick asked, and hoped that she wouldn't say boyfriend or girlfriend. Which was a ridiculous and presumptuous thing to hope, but since when had hope ever been rational?

"I've been invited to a party."

"Must be some party to go halfway around the world."

"Oh, it's very posh. Very VIP. Very special. What about you?"

"I'm on my way to a wedding."

"Ah, they must be good friends if you're traveling halfway around the world."

"Actually, I've met the groom once and the bride never. But he changed my life."

"Once is all it takes." She paused. "Was it for the better or the worse?"

Nick thought of his life. He had achieved his ambitions. He had raced across the Sahara on camelback in Niger. Witnessed the mourning rituals of killer whales from fifty feet away in Alaska. He had been to pockets of the world few knew existed. He'd been happy. And lonely. He loved this life. And he wanted more. Not more career success or money but something else.

"Both," he answered.

"What brought you to Australia?" she asked.

"First rule of journalism is show don't tell," he said, handing her his phone and opening up to the folder where he had loaded a few of his favorite shots from the trip.

She scrolled through. "Surfers," she said, sounding a little disappointed.

"Surfers, but particularly Aboriginal surfers. There's a whole movement of embracing the water as a way to reclaim the ocean and reconnect to the culture after the damage of colonialism."

She smiled and when she did, even her smile lines smiled. She kept scrolling and then stopped on a photo of stones laid out in a circle, against the stark red clay of the Australian outback.

"What's this?"

"That's not for the article."

"What is it?"

"In some indigenous communities, when a person dies, there's a period of mourning when it's forbidden to say the name of the dead or show anything that bears the person's likeness, so they create symbolic representation." He paused. "I got friendly with one of the surfers. He invited me to his family's compound in the outback and told me about it. They call it Sorry Business."

"So you don't have pictures or mention the name of the deceased because it's too painful?" Those glorious smile lines of hers became something else, worry lines, grief. It was a different kind of beauty, but beauty, nonetheless.

"I suppose that could be part of it," Nick replied. "But my friend explained that if you say the name out loud, you might pull the person back into this world. And if you do that, they can't inhabit their next life."

"So it's a way of letting go?"

"I suppose so."

She sighed. "Maybe I should try it. I don't appear to be so good at letting go."

"People in the West struggle with it. Maybe because it's so final for us. We have a thick curtain between life and death. My father's family is Filipino and in that culture, the dead linger for forty days before going to heaven. In other cultures, the ghosts never fully go away; the deceased are more on another plane of existence instead of being gone for good."

"Are you going to do an article on Sorry Business?"

"It's funny you should ask. I'm fascinated with things like this, the way we mark death. The way we leave things behind, seen and unseen, spoken and unspoken. I don't mean to sound morbid, but I've been drawn to things like this for years. It's not my place to write about an Aboriginal spiritual practice, but I've been thinking about inviting people from other cultures to collaborate on a project about mourning rituals, to photograph them, or invite others to photograph them themselves. The way we approach death in the West is so limited, so final, and I think we could stand to learn from other cultures."

He couldn't believe he was telling her this. Chatting with strangers in bars was a fairly normal occurrence for Nick. Telling them about his secretly percolating idea was not.

"I think that sounds beautiful," she said.

I think you're beautiful, Nick thought.

"Announcing the boarding of Qantas flight seven," blared the loudspeaker.

"That's me," he said. He looked at her and had a ridiculous hope. "Is that you, too?"

"I wish," she said. "I had to book my flight last minute, so I have a layover in Singapore and another in Frankfurt."

"Well, it was sweet while it lasted," he said.

"Wasn't it just," she replied.

AMBER

Mom makes one of her lists, divvying up jobs like she used to do with weekend chores, though instead of *vacuum rugs* or *fold laundry*, it contains tasks like *get traveler's checks* and *collect pawnable jewelry.*

"Tomorrow we'll go to church," Mom says, "and announce our departure. And if we can get all our ducks in a row, I'd like to leave Monday."

"But that's Melissa's birthday," I protest. "Why so soon?"

Mom puts a hand on Melissa's shoulder. "It's not going to get any easier."

"So she won't even finish school?" I ask.

"She will, just not here."

I can't even look at Melissa, who has tried to remain her steady, solid self through this, but isn't quite succeeding. I've heard the muffled sobs from her room. I've seen the tear tracks down her face. Of all the horrible things I've done to my sister—and there's quite a count—this one is the worst.

"If you have any goodbyes to make, now's the time," Mom says, looking at Melissa.

Things are better with Mom. I'm not cold all the time. I still don't eat or poop or feel physical sensations. But I know I'm alive somehow, because when my sister's heart breaks, mine does, too.

"I'll go tonight," Melissa says.

After dinner, I pretend to be tired and go to my room. Then I climb out the window and hide in the back seat of the car and wait for Melissa. I'd planned to hide until she got a fair distance away but she isn't going anywhere. She just sits and taps a pen against the blank page of a notebook she brought with her. Finally, she puts the notebook down and backs out the driveway.

"Don't be scared," I say when she turns onto Summit.

"Amber," she says, putting her hand over her heart. "What are you doing here?"

"I came for moral support," I say, climbing into the front seat. "And also I need to say goodbye to Calvin."

"Okay." Melissa looks miserable. I get that offering moral support at the same time as asking for a favor reeks of selfishness—classic Amber—but that's not entirely it. I think I still need to make things right, or righter, with him. Especially if we're leaving.

Melissa's frown deepens. "There's something I need to tell you about Calvin," she says. "I've been going back and forth on it and while I know it might hurt you, I think you should know."

"What is it?"

She takes a deep breath, lets it out. "The reason Dad thought Calvin was guilty was because he acted guilty. He just disappeared. Didn't come to the funeral. Refused to answer any questions about your mood the afternoon of the accident or where he'd been. And he had a black eye that Dad was convinced you gave him in some sort of scuffle."

The thought of me giving Calvin a black eye nearly makes me laugh. It's like a sparrow attacking a grizzly bear.

"Let's say for a minute he knocked me off my bike. It would've been an accident. And anyhow, what does it matter now?" I ask.

"He definitely didn't knock you off your bike. He had an alibi. Corroborated by two other witnesses. Casey Locke and her mother."

"Why would Casey and her mom have anything to do with this?"

As she drives, the streetlights flash across Melissa's face, illuminating her brightly before plunging her back into darkness. "Because they were sleeping together."

"Calvin? Calvin and Casey?"

"Yeah," Melissa replies.

We drive in silence as the betrayal sinks in. It might've been seven years ago but the sting is a fresh wound. My boyfriend was fucking my best friend. My best friend was fucking my

203

boyfriend. I was alive and then I was dead. I was dead and then I was alive. Is nothing in this world true? Is nothing in this world permanent?

"When did it start?" I think back to senior year; if anything, Casey, who'd never loved Calvin, was even nastier about him than ever.

"I don't know the particulars," she replies, "but it was going on when you died."

"How do you know that?"

"Because." She swallows. "Calvin was with Casey when you died."

"They were having sex when I was killed?"

Melissa nods. "I'm sorry." She turns on her indicator light and turns right. "Was it wrong of me to tell you?"

"It was wrong of *them* not to tell me," I fire back, staring out the window at the town I thought I knew. "Correction. It was wrong of them to do it! He said I was his forever love."

"Forever is a long time," Melissa answers. "And people make mistakes." She pauses and looks at me again. "Even good people."

"Was it all just a lie? Did *anyone* love me? Did I matter at all?"

"Of course you did."

"Really? What did I do with my life? Aside from dying?"

"You did plenty. You helped me."

"Just stop!" I put up my hand. "I can't listen to this anymore."

She drives in silence until we get to the turn toward Whittaker.

204

"I changed my mind," I snap. "I don't want to see Calvin ever again."

"Are you sure you don't want to say goodbye?"

"No. Calvin's life has gone to shit. It can stay shit as far as I'm concerned." Any urge I had to help him is erased. He's not my Calvin anymore. Maybe he was never my Calvin. Maybe it was all fake. "Let him suffer."

"I don't think you really mean that."

"You don't? Here's the thing you don't get, Melissa. I'm the last person who deserves a miracle. I've always been a complete bitch."

"Oh, trust me, you're reminding me of that right now," she says, before softening. "I'm sorry. I know this a lot to take in. But this might be your only chance to say goodbye."

Her words hit home. My only chance. "You're right."

She turns on her indicator to go left. "No," I say. "I don't want to see Calvin. There's someone else I need to say goodbye to."

"Who?"

"Dina Weston."

Melissa's mouth opens into an O of surprise.

"I know, I know. We haven't been friends for years, but she's been coming to see me at night. I thought Mom told Detective Weston but I guess Dina found out some other way."

Melissa pulls the car to the side of the road, like Mom used to when we would bicker, refusing to move on until we made peace.

"And in case you're worried that Dina told the Lockes about

me, she didn't. She got mad at me for messaging Casey, same as you."

Melissa still isn't speaking. A truck zooms past, its beams lighting up her face. Her expression is so odd, so peculiar.

"What's wrong?" I ask.

She inhales deeply and then lets it out, as if her breath is deciding something. She turns to me and says, "Dina Weston died four years ago."

MELISSA

Four Years Before

Missy had not been allowed to see Amber's body. She was so broken from the accident, she wasn't even herself anymore, Mom had said. They'd had her cremated.

But when Dina Weston died, there was a body, a viewing. Melissa decided to go and suggested her mother come, too. Perhaps it would help.

"I'm not sure I'm welcome," her mother had said, crying nonstop, as she had been since she'd heard about Dina. Someone from church had told them Dina had died of anaphylactic shock and this had set her mother off. But as it turned out, Dina had not died of an allergic reaction she'd spent her life guarding against but of an aortic aneurysm that no one had seen coming.

"I can't face her," her mother said. "She hates me."

"She doesn't hate you," Missy replied. "She came to Amber's funeral. They both did."

So many people came to pay their respects, but it was Dina who Melissa most remembered. She hadn't seen her in years, not since she and Amber abruptly stopped being friends. Melissa knew the reason why, but she hadn't told anyone. In spite of what Amber thought of her, she'd always been good at keeping secrets.

Amber's friends had been very dramatic at the funeral. Lots of wailing and Ohmygods. Missy knew the feelings were sincere but also like a performance. Dina's distress, on the other hand, had felt all too real. She'd sobbed quietly through the service and then at the reception at their home afterward, she seemed to be struggling. Missy overheard her asking her mother if Amber's clothes were still in the closet, if her toothbrush was still in the bathroom, and Detective Weston kept hushing her, saying, "This is not the appropriate place to have this conversation."

But Missy had immediately understood what Dina was asking: How could a person be gone when they still felt so present?

"Do you want to come to her room?" Missy had asked her at the reception.

"Could I?" Dina asked.

"Sure," she'd replied.

They went down the hall and into Amber's room. The bed was unmade. Brochures for a zip-lining excursion in Mexico Aunt Pauline wanted to take her on were on the nightstand, along with the picture of Amber and Calvin from junior prom. Calvin had not come to the funeral, which had surprised her, but Dina had, which also had surprised her.

"Her stuff is still in the closet?" Dina asked, touching the ruffled hem of the prom dress Amber would never wear. She inhaled. "It still smells like her. Almost like she's still here."

Missy watched. From her years of spying, she had developed a sense of who you could tell things to and who you could not. Amber had not been a confidante before but now was. Dina's mother was someone you could talk to, and so, Missy thought, was Dina.

"She *is* still here," Missy said.

"For real?" Dina asked.

"Not for *real* real. But to me, it seems like she's here. I talk to her all the time."

"You do? What about?"

"That's private," Missy said.

"I understand," Dina said, chastened. She paused to finger her arm of bracelets. "Does she ever talk about me?"

"What do you think she would say?" Missy asked. It was as close as she'd ever come to saying out loud what she knew Amber had done to Dina.

"That's private," Dina had replied.

"I understand," Missy replied. "Mostly she answers my questions, but I can ask her if she has anything to say to you the next time I see her."

"Really?" Dina said. "You can do that?"

"I can and I will," Missy replied.

The promise seemed to bring Dina some comfort. She thanked Missy. "I think I'll go find my mom now."

Dina left for college not long after that and Missy didn't see her again. And now she was gone.

In the end, Melissa could not convince her mother to go to the funeral. And she knew her father wouldn't be welcome after all the trouble he'd given Detective Weston. But the two of them had been compatriots before. Melissa remembered that. So she'd gone alone.

"Thank you for coming, Missy," Detective Weston said, pulling her into a tight hug. "Do you still go by Missy?"

"I go by Melissa now," she said.

"Melissa," Detective Weston repeated, and hugged her again, holding on for a long time. That first time she'd met Dina's mother, Melissa had felt some unspoken understanding between them, even if back then, she'd had no idea why. So she tried to communicate in the silence what she knew. That people could be gone and be here at the same time. You just had to pay attention.

"Would you like to see Dina?" she asked.

Melissa would. She had something to tell her.

Detective Weston led her to the dark wood casket at the front of the sanctuary. Missy peered inside. Dina looked as Missy remembered, except for her hair, which was no longer in the pretty long braids but in equally pretty coiled curls.

Dina's mom was hovering above her. "Do you think I can have a minute alone with her?" Melissa asked.

"Of course."

She ought to have told Dina sooner. She thought she had

more time. But that was the thing, wasn't it? You didn't know. You never knew.

Melissa leaned over so she could speak in Dina's ear, though she knew this was unnecessary. They could hear you no matter where you were. "I asked Amber about you," she whispered. "And she said to tell you that she was really, really sorry."

AMBER

To my sister's credit, she does not freak out that I've been chatting with a dead girl. But then again, she didn't freak out when her dead sister returned.

I, however, am a different story. Because suddenly it's not now, or seven years ago even, but longer. It's a few weeks before middle school graduation. Dina and I are sitting together in the cafeteria. I've unwrapped my sandwich. Dina is picking it up and saying, "What do you have today?" and taking a bite. We'd been eating lunch together for years and she knew that I knew all the rules.

Except that day. I'd broken them. On purpose, never contemplating what would happen. Which was that she took a bite before I could tell her it was a peanut butter sandwich. I'd been warned about the severity of her allergic reactions, but I had never seen one like this. It happened so fast. She started taking these panting breaths. She threw up. She passed out.

She'd stopped bringing her EpiPen with her every day. It was middle school. It was embarrassing. She knew the rules so well. So did I. She could've died. That was what Detective Weston told me after Dina had been rushed to the hospital. Her throat had closed up. They'd had to insert a breathing tube. "She could've died, Amber," her mom told me.

"I didn't mean to. I didn't mean to," I'd cried. And I hadn't meant to hurt her, not like that. But I didn't want to sit with her and only her at lunch anymore. When we went to high school, I wanted to eat with whoever I wanted, make new friends with people who didn't get snickered at in the halls for being weird, who at age thirteen didn't want to still spend weekends galloping around pretending to be horses. I thought that if I ate a peanut butter sandwich while sitting next to Dina, I could trigger a mild reaction. Then, I'd no longer be allowed to sit at the special table. I thought it was a way to tell her without having to say the words that I wanted other friends.

"I didn't mean to," I told her mother a third time.

"I find that hard to believe, Amber," she said. She was a detective. She paid attention.

After that, Dina and I didn't sit at the same table anymore. After that, Dina and I didn't speak anymore.

"Good riddance!" Casey had laughed when I told her the story. By freshman year, I'd upgraded to Casey as a best friend and had convinced myself that the incident with Dina had been an accident. "She was such a loser. You're so much cooler than her."

The shame of it was suffocating. Not just that I'd done it but that some part of me agreed with Casey. I was better off without Dina.

I couldn't tell anyone what I'd done. Not my family, not even Father Mercer during confession. I didn't see how even a merciful God could forgive this.

"Was it—was it an allergic reaction?" I ask Melissa now. The thing with allergies is that they get more severe with every exposure. That peanut butter sandwich I'd given her could have made her next reaction even worse.

"No," Melissa says. "She had an aortic aneurysm. They say she died instantly." She pauses. "Same as you."

Same as me. We had been friends. Best friends. There is no way I'm a miracle. Even before I died, I destroyed things.

"She's dead?" I whisper.

Melissa nods.

"How can I see her?"

My sister shrugs. "How can I see you?"

"Because I'm here. I'm back."

Melissa turns on her indicator light and pulls a U-turn. "You keep asking why I'm so calm about you returning. It's because to me, you never left. You've always been here." Melissa taps her heart. "And here." She taps her head. "I could see you and hear you and talk to you and I could feel you. And it didn't feel like you'd gone away forever so much as moved to a different sort of existence. And you were by my side so much, you helped me so much."

"Me help you? Help anyone? Please, I only make everything worse. I always have. I was always a terrible person. How I was with you. And with Dina . . ." My voice gives out. Shame, it turns out, has a long half-life. "You have no idea what I did to her."

"Of course I do," she says. I stare at her. She raises an arm from the steering wheel. "What can I say, I really was a good spy."

She knows. My sister knows. She has always known. Always paid attention.

"Then how can you even bear to look at me, let alone sacrifice your entire life for me?"

"I'm not sacrificing anything. Nothing is forever. So I don't mind leaving if that's what brings our family back together. And for what it's worth, you *are* a good sister. You weren't always. You screwed up because you were learning, because you were human, but I know you would've figured it out. You did figure it out. You have no idea how much you've helped me these past few years."

"But I was dead!" I cry. "How do you even know you were talking to me? How do you even know I'm back?"

She doesn't answer, just keeps driving. I press my nose to the window and look at our town. It's then I realize we are heading back in the direction we came, back toward home.

"Wait? Don't you want to say goodbye to Lenny?" I ask.

"Not now."

215

"Why not?"

She looks at the blank notebook in her lap. "I don't think I believe in goodbyes."

"What do you mean?"

"You know you asked me how if I've always seen you, how do I know you're actually back now?"

I nod. "Yeah."

She smiles at me. Her eyes are so full of love and also pain. "I don't."

We get to the light at the top of the hill where all sectors of the town are laid out. In one direction is the school, the business Dad spent the last twenty-five years building, the house Mom and Pauline grew up in, the one that Pauline briefly owned but never lived in and then abandoned to Mom as some sort of penance. In another direction is our house, the one Pauline moved to when she was evicted from Gammy's house, the one we all grew up in together. In the other direction is Casey's house. I used to envy her for it, with its three floors, swimming pool, finished basement with a screening room, and her bedroom with the wide canopied bed. Where she was with Calvin the day I died.

In the last direction is Whittaker Court, where Calvin lives.

The sting of the betrayal is already receding, if it was ever there. Like the ember from the fire Dad built that landed on me, it can't truly hurt me now. I'm different, maybe because I was dead and then I wasn't. Or maybe after being dead seven years, I still grew up a little. Or maybe Melissa is right and it's not too late to become a better person. I want to be that better person, to be more like my sister.

"Hey," I say to Melissa, taking hold of her notebook and pen. "Can we make one more stop?"

CALVIN
Five Years Before

He'd always known he was going to hurt her. From that first kiss, he'd known. It was unavoidable. She was planning this forever life for them, but he knew it wasn't going to happen. He was going to ruin it.

That was why he'd applied to that other school, not the one he and Amber agreed to go to together, but the one a thousand miles away. He was surprised when he'd gotten in, more surprised when they'd offered him nearly a full ride if he wrestled for them. And most surprised of all that he wanted to go.

He didn't know how to tell her. He knew that he would hurt her. He'd always known.

And then one day, just before senior year, Casey had texted him to come over. She needed to ask him something. He'd assumed it was something about Amber, so he'd gone. But what Casey had asked him was: "Do you think I'm pretty?"

He should've said no. He should've said, "Doesn't matter what I think because I have a girlfriend I love and you have a best friend you love." But instead, he said yes. And when she'd kissed him, he'd kissed her back.

See? He was fated to hurt Amber. He understood now why Mr. Crane had changed his tune about Calvin. It wasn't that he and Amber had slept together. It was that he'd known who Calvin really was.

His mama worked at the hospital where Amber was brought. She knew first. She called to warn him. The next day when the police came to see him, she rushed home from work.

"Don't you dare question my boy!" she shrieked. "He's a child who just lost the love of his life."

"We aren't questioning him," the policewoman had said, but Calvin could feel her clocking the black eye Casey's father had given him. "We're just trying to see if anyone has any information on the driver."

"He doesn't!" his mama had said. "And he didn't even have the car that day. I did. I was at the hospital. Check the parking lot security footage."

When they left, his mama seemed relieved but Calvin was bereft. He'd wanted to be taken away in cuffs. To be punished.

He didn't go to the funeral. How could he? How could he face her family? They'd known all along.

When the private detective showed up a few years later, wanting to know not just where Calvin had been the afternoon of Amber's death, but who he'd been with, why he hadn't graduated from school or gone on to any of the colleges that had accepted him, Calvin had been relieved. He'd invited the man in. Had brought him to his bedroom, showed him photos of him and Amber, the sheaf of drawings he continued to make of her after her death.

Half an hour into the visit, his mama had come home and found them in Calvin's room. "Who are you ?" she asked, and when the man introduced himself as Earl Simcox and produced a business card reading *Private Detective*, she grew enraged. "Get the hell out of my house. Don't think I don't know why you're after my boy. You got nothing. You aren't even police."

The man left. Calvin wanted to call him back. He wanted to tell someone. So bad. It was eating him alive. Literally. Since Amber had died, he had dropped fifty pounds without so much as trying.

He looked Earl Simcox up online. He was easy to find. Calvin drove out to his office.

The detective seemed surprised—and oddly protective. "Does your mother know you're here?" was the first thing he asked.

"Do you think I killed Amber Crane?" Calvin asked.

Mr. Simcox blanched, as if he'd been singed by shame. Calvin recognized the feeling.

"I'm a private detective. I just do what I'm paid to do."

Calvin told the detective everything. When he finished, he held out his hands in front of him, as he had seen criminals on TV shows do before being handcuffed.

But the detective was not a cop. And he didn't have handcuffs. So when Calvin put his wrists together, ready to fall on the sword, all the detective did was take his shaking wrists in his own hands.

"Son," he said, though they both knew Calvin was not his son, was not any man's son. Never had been, never would be. "Oh, son."

AMBER

While the rest of my family is at church, I make lunch. It's what Dad used to do. Missy, Mom, and I would go to Sunday mass. Dad would stay home and prepare a huge meal. We'd eat and then Mom and Dad would take a nap and Missy and I would finish homework, and that night, we'd have sandwiches or pizza while watching a family movie.

I'm not going all out like Dad would've. No leg of lamb or anything like that. But I bake a cake from a box for Melissa's birthday tomorrow. She's turning seventeen. I'm not letting the day pass without some celebration. As a light rain falls outside, I dig out some chicken breasts from the freezer and apricot marmalade from the pantry. I defrost the chicken, caramelize some onions, mix them with the jam, spread the mixture over the chicken, and add a few shakes of paprika. I have not made this recipe in years, apparently, but it comes back to me. I can't smell it, not really, but I can imagine the aroma greeting my family, the comfort of a waiting hot meal.

It's funny the things you take for granted. Sunday lunch with your family. This is something I've always had so I didn't notice it. But now I do. Now I notice everything. Like Melissa, I'm learning to pay attention. Because clearly I wasn't before. Calvin and Casey. How could I have missed that?

The anger has passed now. I loved Calvin once. We said it was forever but as I wrote him in my letter, I'm not even sure what forever means, what time means, or even what death means. To Melissa I'm alive. I've always been alive. Then again, my sister is special. She always was. I just wasn't paying the right attention to understand that.

I'm frosting the cake when Mom's car pulls into the driveway. I fluff the rice and check the chicken. I pull plates from the cabinet and start to set the table.

"Wow, it smells amazing in here," Melissa calls as she comes inside.

"Amber, are you cooking?" Mom asks, shaking off her umbrella. The rain has started to come down heavier now.

"Yeah," I say, feeling oddly shy around my family. "I made Sunday lunch." I give the frosting a final swirl. "And birthday cake."

"A real celebration," Dad says, his eyes shining.

Mom takes over the table-setting for me. Not with the regular plates but the wedding china that she only uses for special occasions. She extracts the beeswax taper candles she buys from an apiarist on the edge of town and lights them.

"This is really nice," Melissa says as we sit down at the table, the four of us, like we used to do.

"Thank you. Happy birthday."

"Not until tomorrow," she says.

"Is it weird that we'll both be seventeen?" I pause. "Am I seventeen? Or am I twenty-four?"

"These are all details we can work out later," Mom says. She takes a piece of chicken from the tray and is about to pass it to me, but then she looks at me for a long moment and passes it to Melissa.

It's a little thing, but from Mom it means a lot. She knows there's something not right with me. But she's accepting me for what I am.

Dad's phone chimes. He picks it up and frowns before turning it off.

"Who was it?" Mom asks.

"It's that reporter again. He's in town. He asked if we could meet."

He looks at Mom, as if bracing for her anger. But she picks up the rice, passes it to Melissa, and says, "Don't you hate it when people call during mealtimes?"

"It's the worst!" Melissa agrees, and they all laugh.

"It seems like church went well," I say.

"It did," Mom says.

"It was good," Dad adds. "Nice. It felt right to be there. Together."

"Maybe we can find a church that has room for lesbians and atheists who believe in miracles and God," Mom jokes.

"I think that's the Unitarians," Melissa quips.

"I don't need church to confirm what I believe in," Dad says. "I just need this family. I believe in us."

"Me too," Mom says, and they brush hands, like they used to.

"Did you make an announcement?" I ask. "Were people suspicious?"

"Not really," Mom says. "We met with Father Mercer ahead of time and told him we got back together."

"And that this was the miracle," Dad says.

"And he agreed it was," Mom says.

"Then we told him we would be traveling for the next few weeks for family matters," Dad says.

"He didn't blink," Mom says. "I don't think he told Scott Locke."

"So maybe we don't have to leave?" I look at Melissa.

Diplomatic as always, my sister changes the subject. "Mom and Dad weren't the only ones getting a blessing. You'll never guess who else is getting married."

"Who?"

"Remember Mr. King from school?"

"The English teacher?" I ask.

Melissa nods.

"How is he still alive?" I ask. "He was like eighty when I died."

"He was in his sixties," Dad says. "And he's alive and well and recently retired from teaching."

"He's marrying a very nice woman who used to volunteer at the pet shelter. I can't recall her name," Mom adds.

"Kinda late to get married," I say.

Mom and Dad touch hands. "There's no such thing as too late," Dad says.

ARNOLD
Fifteen Minutes Earlier

No one knew exactly how old Barley was. The vet esti-
mated between eight and ten when Nancy adopted him.
That was five years ago, which put him somewhere between
thirteen and fifteen—nearly one hundred in dog years. He was
old. His kidneys were failing. He was blind and could no longer jump onto the couch. His hair was so matted that Lady had
taken to grooming him.

He was dying.

His impending death had opened a hole of grief in Nancy,
who found herself mourning, all these years later, the loss of her
son, Jeremy.

Family was precious. It was a lesson Arnold had learned late
in life, but he understood it deeply. The dog was family. And
Jeremy was family. One had left Nancy; the other would soon
leave.

He had sold his house a few years back when he'd moved in with Nancy and had a nice nest egg from that. He used a large chunk of it on an engagement ring. The practical side of him knew that spending this much on a ring for a marriage that would, according to actuarial tables, last ten years if they were lucky, was silly. But he didn't care. Love was love. Family was family. This mattered.

Three months earlier, he'd gotten down on bended knee— no small feat for an arthritic seventy-one-year-old—and asked Nancy to marry him.

They decided to do it in early May. Before it got too hot was how they put it. But the subtext was there. Before Barley passed. In preparation, they came up with a guest list. Hired out a restaurant. They bought Barley a tuxedo collar and Lady a taffeta one, which she ripped to shreds the minute they put it on her. And Arnold hired a detective.

Over the years, he'd raised the idea of looking for Jeremy, but Nancy always refused. "If he wants to come home, he knows where to find me."

In the end, he decided to go against his fiancée's wishes for two reasons. The first was that it turned out that Arnold had taught Jeremy. He hadn't remembered him but when he'd moved in with Nancy, they'd cleaned out her attic and he'd come across Jeremy's old notebooks—and there among the papers was his obituary assignment. The last lines struck him: *Jeremy Halyard lived a long life. In the end, he surprised everyone. Especially himself.*

He thought about that obituary often these days. He wanted

to give the boy a chance to surprise himself. He now knew, of course, that Jeremy had a drug problem. Had had one as far back as high school when he'd written that assignment.

The second reason he decided to look for Jeremy was that he knew that losing Barley was going to carve a chasm in Nancy that he wasn't sure he alone could fill.

So he hired a local detective named Earl Simcox, who gave him an address where the young man was living. He printed out a wedding invitation and put it in the mail. Every day he went to the mailbox to look for a response. Every day he checked the email account they'd set up for RSVPs. He heard from his old friend Nick Flores, who emailed that he would be coming. He heard from his cousin, who said that he would not. He heard from Nancy's friends she'd made over the years at the pet shelter, where she'd gone from volunteer to manager to retiree. But he hadn't heard from Jeremy.

The wedding was this week. Just that morning at church, Father Mercer had called up Arnold and Nancy for a benediction. And he'd also called up another couple for theirs, a husband and wife who'd separated and reunited. He hadn't recognized them. His eyesight wasn't what it once was, after all those years of marking papers. He was always losing his glasses. He had left them in the car that day.

It was Nancy who recognized them. "I think that's her."

"Who?" Arnold whispered.

"The woman who was supposed to adopt Barley. But she was too upset about losing her cat." Nancy paused. "Mr. Fluff. That had been the cat's name. I can't believe it came to me after all these years."

Though he had told Nancy so much about his past, he had never told her about Amber and therefore that he'd also recognized Gloria Crane that day they met. It felt like an intrusion into the family's privacy and honestly, it was something he grappled with. He often thought of that quote he'd suggested to the principal for Amber's memorial wall, that someone had to die for everyone to live more. He'd had no way then of knowing how Amber's death would, inadvertently, lead him to Lady, to Barley, and to Nancy. How it would bring him to his family. It would give him his life.

He sometimes wondered how the family would react to knowing this. Would they resent that they had paid the price for his happiness? Or be glad that their daughter's death had changed his life for the better? But he never thought about asking them, just chalked this up to another of life's mysteries that would go unanswered.

On the way home from church, Arnold and Nancy stopped to run a few errands: finalizing the flowers, picking up the lanterns they were going to string on the bushes outside the restaurant. It was coming on two by the time they arrived home, and both were worn out.

It had rained that afternoon. A branch had fallen off the maple tree, blocking the driveway.

"I'll get it," he told Nancy. "You take Barley out." The poor guy couldn't hold his bladder as long as he could when he was younger.

"Thank you," Nancy said, kissing him lightly on the cheek.

He parked on the street, behind an unfamiliar car. He was just starting to clear the branch when Nancy screamed.

She was standing at the open front door. Arnold's first thought was that it was the dog. Barley had died, days before their wedding.

But then Barley ambled outside, peeing on the first bush he saw before he trotted over to Arnold, pressing his button nose into Arnold's knees. Arnold turned to Nancy to see what the matter was just as a man emerged from the dark house.

AMBER

After the meal is finished, I go into the kitchen and put seventeen candles on the cake.

Happy birthday, we sing. I put the cake in front of Melissa. She takes a deep breath and blows out the candles.

"What did you wish for?" I ask.

"You know I can't tell you that," Melissa says with a sneaky smile that reminds me so much of Missy.

They eat the cake and then I start to clear. "Wait," Mom says, gesturing for me to sit back down.

She and Dad look at each other. They clasp hands as Mom says, "Father Mercer asked if we wanted to renew our vows since we never technically got divorced." They look at each other and smile.

"We can't do that, not in front of the congregation, but I thought we might do something in front of you girls." Dad reaches into his pocket and pulls out a thin silver band. Mom opens her palm and there's another one.

I have never seen the rings anywhere but on my parents' hands. They never took them off, not to wash dishes or to work the cement mixer. If they ever did, Melissa and I vowed we would swipe them, only for a minute, just to see what top secret message was engraved inside.

I look at Melissa. She's looking at me. I know we're thinking the same thing. *This is our chance.*

Mom hands Melissa her ring and Dad hands me his. They stand up. They giggle awkwardly, and I can see them for the college students they once were. So young and willing to take this big leap of faith. Not everyone makes it across. They almost didn't.

"I love you, Brian," Mom says. "I always have. I always will. And I won't let anything life throws at me muddy that again. We are each other's forevers. And I will love you forever."

Dad's eyes are wet as he takes Mom's hand. "I've always believed in miracles, Gloria," he said. "Because that's how I found you."

I turn to Melissa, who is smiling with her whole heart and I know even if she'll never tell me, this is what she wished for.

They look at us. "Rings, please," they say.

I almost forgot! I glance quickly at the engraving and almost laugh. We'd thought it was some grand mystery, but they've been saying it all along.

BRIAN
Twenty-Six Years Before

The wedding had gone by in a blur. His mother had warned him it would, but he hadn't expected how time would contract and snap like that, and one minute he would be in the all-purpose room of the church, helping Pauline clasp on a necklace, and the next minute, he and his bride would be sitting on the folding chairs looking around the empty banquet hall full of plates smeared with cake frosting and flowers now wilting in their vases. The last guest had left. The deejay had packed up. The waiters were clearing the remaining dishes and pulling off the white polyester tablecloths.

They weren't going on a honeymoon. Not with Gloria's father so sick and their decision to save for a down payment on a house. Instead, they were spending the night at the Red Lion Inn where, with help from Pauline, Brian had decorated the walls with tear-outs from travel magazines of all the places they would go one day, an idea he had shamelessly stolen from *It's a Wonderful Life*.

Still in their wedding gown and tux, but barefoot now, they made their way to the parking lot. Brian's car was in the corner spot he'd left it at, six hours and another lifetime ago. They were married now. Their lives were forever linked. At his bachelor party, a tame affair at the bowling alley, his friends had teased him for being yoked to a woman at the ripe old age of twenty-two. He'd hardy-harred along with them but didn't tell them the truth. That the idea of being joined with Gloria forever made him inexplicably happy. It was all he wanted.

They drove to the hotel and he unlocked the door. Brian carried Gloria over the threshold and the two of them gasped.

The plan had been for Pauline to put up a dozen or so pictures: London, Paris, New York. But she had papered the walls with travel images of places both familiar—the Sydney Opera House—and less so, the temples of Samarkand.

"Pauline went a little overboard," Brian said.

"For Pauline, this is tame!" Gloria replied.

She was laughing as he kissed her. Kissed his wife.

"It gives us something to aim for. See the world," Brian said.

"I don't care about seeing the world. As long as I'm with you, that is my world."

Brian fingered his wedding band, the same style as Gloria's. One day, he would buy her the diamond she deserved.

"Did you see what I had engraved in the rings?" she asked.

"I didn't know you had them engraved."

She smiled and his heart ached. Oh, she was so beautiful, this woman, and now she was his wife. Until death do them part.

"I know. I wanted to surprise you earlier but in all the hustle and bustle, I forgot." She started to pull her own ring off. "I had them both engraved with the same thing. I hope you like it."

Brian twisted his ring off and stared at his hand. He'd worn the band for only a few hours but already his hand felt naked without it.

He glanced at the inside of it. The writing was so tiny he had to squint to make it out.

My Miracle, it said.

He put the ring on, vowing never to take it off again.

AMBER

Melissa and I do dishes as Mom and Dad decide what things we can and can't take with us. Nearly everything will get left behind.

"Easy for me," I tell Melissa. "I don't own anything."

"The old Amber would've brought like ten trunks," Melissa says, rinsing off a plate and handing it to me to load in the dishwasher. "You hated to get rid of anything. Remember the time Mom emptied your wastebasket and you flipped out?"

"Because Calvin's T-shirt was in there."

"Which you'd thrown out," Melissa says.

"Because we were in a fight. It was a dramatic gesture."

"What were you fighting about?"

"I can't even remember," I say. "But one thing about being dead for seven years is that it really shifts your perspective."

"Helps get your priorities straight," Melissa jokes.

"See the world in a new light."

"More people should try it."

"Cheaper than therapy."

We giggle. Two sisters being goofy. For a moment, everything feels so right.

And then the doorbell rings.

"Who is that?" Mom calls, her own voice ringing in alarm.

Melissa peers out the kitchen window. "It's Scott Locke," she says in a shout-whisper. "With Casey," she adds.

"Shit!" I dive toward Melissa's old cubby hidey-hole.

"Don't answer the door!" Mom hisses.

"He already saw us," Dad whispers. "It'll be more suspicious if we don't. Just stay calm."

He walks to the front hall, opens the door. "Scott," he says, his voice booming and cheerful. "How nice to see you. And you, Casey. Wow, how long has it been?"

From my hiding spot, I can see Mom. The look of terror is exactly the same expression she wore when she saw me again. Melissa goes to her, puts a hand on her shoulder.

"Hi, Mr. Crane." Casey sounds nervous. And she looks it, too. Underneath her pretty blond hair, her suntan, she looks scared. I should hate her. Or be angry. But I can't be. If I forgive Calvin, I have to forgive her.

"Mind if we come in?" Mr. Locke asks.

"We're actually in the middle of something," Dad says.

"Yes, I can see that. Looks like you're packing or something."

I hear the sound of footsteps as Casey's father enters. Casey shuffles in behind him.

"We are," Dad says. "I'm moving back in, you see, and so we're doing a purge before we consolidate households."

"Yes, I heard about that. Congratulations on your happy union." He puts such an emphasis on *congratulations*, it sounds sarcastic. "I also heard you're leaving town for a while."

"How'd you hear that?" Mom asks in a tremulous voice.

"You announced it to the whole church. It's the best way to spread gossip in this town. Tell the faithful."

"We're having some family issues," Dad says.

"Family issues," Mr. Locke says. "You've had a lot of those, haven't you?"

Mom gasps. Even from someone like Scott Locke, this is a low blow.

"We've had our share," Dad says, his voice growing tight.

"Well, what's that they say? God never gives you more of a load than you can carry?" And then Scott chuckles. His laughter is like metal against metal. It makes even Melissa flinch.

"What can I do for you, Scott?" Dad says, his voice growing angry.

"If you remember, my daughter raised those funds for your family."

"Yes, that was very thoughtful of you, Casey."

"Thank you," Casey says in a quiet voice.

"It *was* very thoughtful. And very generous. People opened their hearts for you. And their wallets. Raised quite a bit of money, didn't it?"

"It did."

"Nearly two hundred thousand dollars. How was that money spent?"

"That's not really your business, Scott."

"Well, it kind of is. My daughter raised it."

"Without telling us," Mom calls out. "We never asked for that money. And we didn't need it. It caused more trouble than it was worth."

"Gloria," Dad says, trying to calm her with a lowering of his hands before turning back to Scott. "We appreciate Casey's generosity but as the money was not solicited, and as no conditions were put on its use, we haven't done anything wrong."

"That's just the thing," Scott drawls in an almost playful tone. He's enjoying this, the way a cat will play with a captured mouse before killing it. "You haven't done anything wrong if Amber is actually dead, but is she?"

Mom lets out a cry and puts her hands over her mouth.

"Of course she's dead," Dad says, but he doesn't sound so convincing.

"Here's the odd thing. Casey got a call from Calvin Judd, that old boyfriend, and he said that he saw Amber, he spoke to her."

"That boy is troubled," Dad says in a choked voice.

"He's a druggy loser is what you mean. Such a shame. But not a shocker." Scott's tone is casual and sadistic.

I try to grab a better glimpse of Casey. She had to grow up with this? Why hadn't she told me? Why hadn't I noticed?

"Still, he swore he saw her, twice in fact," Scott continues, "and then Casey got a note from your daughter here asking to get in touch with Calvin. It all seems a little suspicious."

"What exactly did Calvin tell you?" Dad asks Casey.

"Uh—uh," Casey stutters. But before she answers, there's another knock at the door.

The hinge squeaks open and Casey's father laughs again. "Speak of the devil," he says.

CASEY
Now

As soon as she sees Calvin, Casey regrets coming.

No, that's not entirely true. There'd been that niggling warning anxiety in her stomach ever since she told her dad about Calvin's strange call and the message from Amber's sister.

"I smell a rat and we're going to smoke this out together," her father had said.

Casey didn't believe that Amber had come back from the dead, obviously. And she didn't really think the Cranes had faked her death, either. But her father was so emphatic about her coming, about salvaging the family's reputation—her reputation. Plus, he'd already bought her a plane ticket, business class. So she ordered a car to the airport and flew home. Her dad was waiting at baggage claim, something he hadn't done for ages.

"You'll never believe this," he said as they peeled onto the expressway. "But according to your mother's friend Cathy, the Cranes were in church this morning, even the father, who never goes."

"I thought they split up," Casey said. Her mother had reported this to her years ago, almost gleefully. No one saw that coming, she'd texted, and Casey could hear the words in the same gossipy tone that she felt sure people employed to snipe about the Lockes.

"I thought a lot of things," her father replied. "But you haven't even heard the most damning part of all." He shook his head and squeezed the steering wheel so tight the padded leather sighed under his grip. "The Cranes are going away for a few months to tend to family matters. Family matters! Can you believe that crock of shit?"

Her father laughed, like attending to family matters was for chumps.

The hard kernel of unease that had sat in Casey's belly since she'd called her father seemed to grow, a tumor swelling into a boulder. It would flatten her from the inside out.

As they pulled into Amber's driveway, Casey's knees were shaking. What if Amber *was* there? What if she was alive? What if she knew about what Casey had done to her? She talked such a big game about not caring if Amber found out about her and Calvin, but a weird silver lining of her death was that it had guaranteed she never would find out.

When Mr. Crane opened the door, Casey nearly turned around and ran away. This man had always been kind to her, adding extra chocolate chips to her pancakes on mornings that she slept over because she'd told him that her mother would never allow chocolate with breakfast (too fattening!). And his explanation about all the boxes, that he and Mrs. Crane were getting back together, it sounded legit to her.

But now Calvin shows up. Screaming, "Amber, Amber!" and waving a piece of paper in his hand, and all that sadness and regret metastasizes into fury.

Amber. It's always about Amber. It's always been about Amber. What was so special about her? She was cute enough and smart enough and had a good singing voice but she wasn't going to Broadway or anything. She was just some average girl in some average town with some average boyfriend. If she hadn't died young, she would've faded into oblivion like the rest of them.

When Calvin sees Casey, he skids to a halt, his mouth ajar. He has the gall to look right at her, to ask: "Have you seen Amber? Is she here?"

Casey's father turns to Mr. Crane. "You heard what the boy said. Is she here?"

"Of . . . of course she's not here," Mr. Crane says.

"What you got there?" her father asks, gesturing to the paper in Calvin's hand.

"A letter." Calvin's voice is hoarse, his eyes are wild. "She wrote me." He looks at the paper and reads in a staccato, almost manic, voice:

"Dear Calvin. I don't know what forever means anymore because I'm not sure time works the way we think it does or even life or death means what we think it does. But I think love does. Because no matter where I have been or where I am going I know that I love you. I feel that with a certainty I can't explain. And no matter what you have done or what you think you have done, I love you. I feel that with a certainty, too. Loving someone, really loving someone, means wanting them to be whole and happy and free, with you or without you. I don't think I understood that before but I do now. If you love me, if you ever loved me, please live a whole life, a happy life, and a free life. Yours, forever, Amber."

Calvin finishes reading and collapses into sobs while Casey's father laughs. "I'd call that a smoking gun, wouldn't you?" And in that moment Casey's fury shifts and lands right on her father. This man she looked up to, this man she needed. She would hate him, but she's not sure she loves him enough to hate him.

"No, I'd call that a young man in pain," Mr. Crane says, and then he gathers Calvin into his arms. Calvin is so much skinnier than he used to be, but he's still tall and he flops over Mr. Crane like a tired toddler as silent sobs rack his emaciated body.

"I've got you, son," Mr. Crane murmurs. "I got you." And then he, too, starts to cry.

Casey's father whips out his phone. "I'm calling the police."

"Dad, leave it," Casey says. "Just leave it."

"I already called Detective Weston," Melissa says, wielding her phone in her hand like a weapon. "She's on her way."

And then Melissa also embraces Calvin. "I'm sorry," she says. "We shouldn't have left you all alone."

And then Mrs. Crane is there, too. The three of them stand in the foyer, comforting Calvin.

And Casey, she's suddenly sick of them all. Sick of being jealous of Amber, sick of Calvin, the Cranes. Wanting what she hasn't got. Having what she doesn't need.

"I'm done," she says, turning to go. She pushes past Calvin, down the walk, eyes on her phone, already summoning a car to get the hell out of here and never, ever come back. At the edge of the sidewalk, she nearly smacks into a tall, thin Black woman with short-cropped graying hair who she vaguely remembers as the mother of that weird girl Amber used to hang out with. The cop who confirmed Calvin had been with her when Amber died. She probably hated Casey. Everyone in this town did.

But the woman's voice is kind. "Casey," she says. "Are you okay?"

"I gotta get out of here," she says. Black spots are dancing before her eyes. She feels drunk. Dizzy.

"Okay. First, I want you to sit down."

The detective takes Casey gently by the elbow and leads her back up the walk to a wooden bench on Amber's porch. "Put your head between your legs and breathe."

The front door is still open. Casey can still hear her father arguing with Mr. Crane. "What seems to be the issue?"

246

Detective Weston calls into the house, never removing the hand from Casey's shoulder.

From the dark space between her legs, Casey listens to her father's insane rant: The Cranes faked Amber's death to steal the money their family raised, only to trash his family's reputation. He'd been drafted to run for city council but after this whole business, no one wanted him around. They were pariahs. And the Cranes were the real criminals. The detective listens quietly, giving Casey's shoulder a little squeeze, as if to tell her she knows this isn't Casey speaking, she absolves Casey, at least from this.

"She's not even dead! The boy saw her. Just ask," her father is yelling.

"Calvin," Detective Weston says. "Have you heard from Amber?"

"Yes," he gasps. "She came to see me the other day and she wrote me this letter." He waves the paper at Detective Weston and all of a sudden he gasps. "She's here. I see her! She's in the kitchen."

Casey forces herself to look up as Calvin moves from the foyer toward the kitchen. She stands up. If Amber is really here, she'll face it. That's the least she can do.

"Amber," Calvin cries as he runs toward the kitchen. Detective Weston follows, bringing Casey with her.

"Okay, where is she, Calvin?" Detective Weston asks, gesturing toward the kitchen counter where Calvin is holding his arms tightly around himself.

"Amber," Calvin keeps saying.

"I don't see anyone, Calvin," the detective says.

"There was a letter," Casey's father shouts. "He just read it."

He snatches the piece of paper from Calvin's grip and without looking at it, hands it to Detective Weston. Casey is right next to her so she can peer over the detective's shoulder to look at it.

The paper is blank.

AMBER

Calvin is holding me tight, crying, calling my name over and over. He holds me as Dina's mom ushers Casey's father outside, telling him in a quiet voice that our family has had enough grief by now and if the harassment continues, she'll have him arrested.

Calvin continues holding me as Mom turns to Detective Weston. "She's here, Peg. Can you see her?"

Detective Weston shakes her head. "I can't. But I'm so glad you can. You've missed her so much."

"I've missed her so much that I couldn't let myself remember her because I thought it would be too painful, but she is here and I love her. I love my girl so much!" Mom starts to cry.

"I know," Detective Weston says, crying now, too. "I love *my* girl so much. Every single day that love keeps me going, too. That love never dies. It lives in us forever."

My mom and Dina's mom hold each other, pulling Melissa into the embrace. I'm right there but Detective Weston doesn't see me. Just like Casey and her dad didn't see me. Because they didn't need to see me.

I'm back, and I'm not.

I died and yet I stayed alive.

I'm here and I'm leaving.

I turn Calvin away from me. I push him toward my family. My family has so much love. When I left, my parents didn't know what to do with it all. It curdled. But love needs to be spent, lavished, not squandered.

My father grips Calvin again. "We see her," he says to Calvin. "We see her, too."

And then they're all crying again, hugging each other, in grief and in joy and in togetherness. I stand to the side. I hear my father say to Calvin, "I'm so sorry we never did that fishing trip. Summer's coming. Maybe we should make a plan."

Calvin wipes his eyes. "I'd like that, sir."

Detective Weston puts her arm around Calvin and leads him out of the house, murmuring something into his ear. He slumps into her and I get the feeling that Calvin is going to be all right. That my whole family is going to be all right.

NICK
Ten Minutes After

Nick was never good at sleeping on planes. The years of travel have not improved matters, so by the time he arrives at the Crane residence, it's been two days since he last slept.

So when he sees her, the woman from the airport in Sydney, emerge from a taxi in front of the same house he's just parked his rental car in front of, he assumes he's hallucinating. He had spent the long flight regretting not getting her number or email address or even last name so he could track her down. And now he's hallucinating her.

But if he is, it's a very realistic vision because it's laughing and crying and waving at him.

"What are you doing here?" Nick manages to sputter.

"I'm here for the party," she replies. "What are *you* doing here?"

"I've been trying to get in touch with the family, the Cranes and—" He stops himself, remembering her beautiful sadness. What was it she'd said in the airport when he'd told her about Sorry Business? *I don't appear to be so good at letting go.*

"Amber Crane was your . . . ?" Nick trails off.

"My niece. But also like my sister. We grew up together. Her mother, Gloria, practically raised me. I haven't seen her . . ." Now it's her voice that breaks.

Nick takes her hand and clasps it, and something in his restless spirit stills.

She squeezes his hand back. "Do you want to go to a party?"

"I'd love to," he says.

She rings the bell. It opens. A woman opens the door. Amber's mother. Nick sees the resemblance immediately.

"Gloria," she says as Gloria says, "Pauline."

Pauline. Her name is Pauline.

Pauline and her sister hug for a long time, crying and laughing in each other's arms. Nick has long grown accustomed to being an observer of such things, but usually the lens allows a barrier between himself and this intimacy, this messy thing called life. But now he doesn't have his camera and he doesn't want to hide. He wants to dive in. To all of it.

And then, another car pulls up and out steps Arnold King.

Okay, he *must* be hallucinating.

"Arnold!" he calls. "Is that you?"

"Nick?" Arnold replies. "What are *you* doing here?"

Just then the back door of Arnold's car opens and out steps a woman, silver curly hair, a kind face. This, he knows, is Nancy.

252

From the other door emerges a man younger than Nick but who seems, in his stooped demeanor, older than Arnold.

The younger man spots the house and leans over to retch into a patch of rosebushes alongside the driveway.

Both women recognize the change in the air. "What's going on?" Pauline asks.

"Miracles! Brian, come here," Gloria calls.

Brian steps out, followed by a young woman with short blue hair who squeals when she sees Pauline and hugs her.

Then, Pauline once again takes his hand.

The young woman turns toward the driveway. "Mr. King?" she asks.

"Yes, hello, Melissa," Arnold says, and Nick can hear in his voice the teacher he once was. "Brian, Gloria," he says, nodding at the Cranes.

One of the things that makes Nick such a good photographer is this sense for when things are about to happen, a surfer about to emerge from the maw of a forty-foot curl, a sunrise about to explode. And he knows this is one of those moments. He stands still, he pays attention, he holds on to Pauline's hand.

Arnold steps forward, along with the woman and the terrified-looking man. "This is Nancy Halyard, my soon-to-be wife, and this is her son, and I suppose in a way, soon to be my son, Jeremy."

AMBER

I recognize him the minute I see him. I haven't thought about him before, haven't remembered it before, but now I do. I can remember the rust of his bumper, the squeal of his tires, the look of pure horror as I somersaulted over the windshield of his car. I remember the punch of his breath as he got out to look at me. The touch of his hand against my already-quiet pulse. The awful gasp of his sob. And the draft of his car as he drove away.

My father strides toward him. "Hello, Jeremy." He offers his hand but Jeremy doesn't take it. He holds his arms stiff to his side as if shackled.

Then he speaks. "I'm the one who did it. I'm the one who killed your daughter. I'm so sorry. I've been sorry every day of my life. If I could go back in time and change places with her, I would. If I could give my life now to bring her back, I would. But I can't."

At this, Dad's gaze scans for me. He lands in my general direction. Blinks once, blinks twice. Melissa walks over and takes my hand.

"I want you to know I had no idea," Nancy cuts in, hand over her heart. "Back then, he was an addict. He wasn't living at home. I hadn't even known he was back in town when it happened. I only found out this afternoon. He'd been coming home when he hit the girl. He'd been coming home to try to get better. I didn't know. I wouldn't have kept that from you. I know how hard it is to lose a child."

Her voice breaks.

Dad looks back to where I'm standing with Melissa. He looks back to the crying woman.

"He turned his life around," Nancy continues. "He's sober now. He's married and he's studying to be a nurse, so he can help people."

Dad looks at me again, squinting.

Pauline stands holding that man's hand but she doesn't seem to see me.

"Why are you telling us this now?" Dad asks Jeremy.

"I've wanted to tell you every day for the past seven years," Jeremy says. "But I was too much of a coward and I made up excuses, like it wouldn't bring her back, or I could do more good helping others, but really, I was just too scared. And now, I got a kid on the way."

At this Nancy cries out, covers her mouth with her hands. Mr. King leans over and kisses her.

"Yeah, Ma," Jeremy says. "A girl. She's due in August."

Mom and Dad look at each other. I was a girl, born in August.

"And the thing is, I don't want my kid coming into this world with a father like me. I keep imagining how I'd feel if someone did this to her. She's not even born yet and I can tell it would rip me to shreds. It's shameful what I did. The accident was an accident, but the not coming forward, I chose to do that. So when I got word that Ma was getting married, I knew I had to come back. My wife says if this is what I gotta do to be a good father, then I gotta do it."

He falls to his knees before Dad. "I wanna be a good father. I wanna be a father worthy of my daughter. Tell me what to do."

Dad looks to Mom, who reaches out her hand to hold his; her other hand holds Pauline, who is holding the hand of a man who's her boyfriend or maybe her husband.

"Stand up," Dad orders.

Jeremy stands up, wiping his eyes with his sleeve.

"I'll turn myself in right now. Or you can call the police," Jeremy says.

"I think we've had enough police for the day." Dad scans the yard, looking at the rosebushes Mom planted for all of us, the cul-de-sac where he taught me to ride a bike, to the front door he carried Mom across, then me in my baby seat, then Melissa. This time, he doesn't see me, but I think he knows what I want him to say, what I would say.

"Here's what I want you to do, Jeremy," Dad says in a choked voice. "I want you to love that daughter of yours with all your heart. I want you to be there for her and for your wife even when things get so hard you don't think you can walk another step. Can you do that for me, Jeremy?"

There's a brief pause before Jeremy answers, and in the silence I hear everything: babies crying and bicycle bells ringing and hands clapping and lips kissing and waves lapping and crickets chirping and choirs singing and all the sounds of life, life, life.

And then Jeremy answers. "Yes, sir. I believe I can."

MELISSA
Now

Melissa gets Amber's bike from the back of the garage where her father had hidden it. Is it a bike? Has it really been hidden? These distinctions never mattered much to Melissa. Seeing something is not the same as believing, and believing something does not always require seeing.

Her mom has sent Aunt Pauline inside with her boyfriend, both of them delirious with exhaustion, to rest. It's just the immediate family as Melissa wheels the bike out front.

"Is she gone?" her mother asks Melissa.

"Am I gone?" Amber asks Melissa.

Amber is standing next to her. But Amber has always been next to her.

"I still see her," Melissa says.

"Will you tell her that I'm going to be okay?" Mom says. "I didn't think I could stand losing her again but I'm not, not really losing her this time. I'll keep her close, like you've done, Melissa."

"Tell her I heard that," Amber says. "That I love her. I'll always love her."

"She heard that," Melissa says. "She loves you. She'll always love you."

Her mom starts to sob but it's a different tenor than it has been all these years, not choked in grief but laced in joy, because love and loss are the flip sides of the same coin. She's grieving Amber because she lost her, but she's not entirely losing her because she loves her.

"Did you always know I wasn't going to stay?" Amber asks.

Melissa wasn't sure until Amber told her that she'd seen Dina. Then she knew. It was why she didn't break up with Lenny. Well, part of it. She really didn't believe in goodbyes. People stayed around so long as you kept them close.

"I guess I wasn't really a miracle," Amber says.

Melissa disagrees. If you pay attention, you see that miracles are everywhere. In a sunrise. In a bicycle accidentally locked to another. In the way that memory and love and belief can keep a person around long after they're gone.

She hands her sister the bicycle. Amber takes it.

"I'll see you soon," Melissa tells her, because she will, as she always has.

And then she takes her mother and father by the hand and walks them back into the house.

AMBER

I pedal back out of the driveway. Three houses down at the end of the cul-de-sac I know I will find Dina. She's sitting on her front lawn, picking at a yellow dandelion, waiting for me.

I get off my bike. And then I tell her, "I'm sorry."

It's so easy to say. Why did I wait so long?

"That's okay," she says.

"Can we be friends again?"

"I thought we already were." She looks toward the house, where Detective Weston and another woman, Kathy, I guess, are in the kitchen talking.

"Will I see you again? In the, whatever?"

"You see me now. Isn't this the, whatever?"

"I guess you're right." I climb back on my bike. "I think I have to go now."

She nods. "I'm going to stick around a bit." She plucks a

potato bug from the grass; it crawls up her arm and she watches it with awe. I leave her like that.

I push off on my bike. I pedal past my house, Dad's truck next to Mom's car in the driveway. I pedal past my ghost bike, past the place where I left this life.

I get to the top of the hill. From here the town is spread out in front of me. Somewhere out there is the high school, and the kids who will walk past the mural of me, heading toward futures still unknown. Somewhere out there is Mr. King, about to get married. Somewhere out there is Lenny, who will celebrate Melissa's birthday with her tomorrow. Somewhere out there is Calvin with his composition book in his lap, drawing pictures. Somewhere out there is life, starting and ending and ending and starting.

Melissa was right. Life. Death. We don't know. We can never know. We can just have faith.

I pause at the crest, in that perfect moment, the feather suspended in the air. It's downhill from here. I push myself off, letting go of the handlebars, raising my hands to my side. I feel light as air. The wind whips under my arms, so strong like it might lift me off this bike, like it might carry me home.

AFTER WORD

In Judaism, when a person dies, it's customary to say to the bereaved "May their memory be a blessing." I always loved this. Whereas telling someone "Sorry for your loss" feels a little useless and empty, the Jewish refrain feels instructive for how to survive the loss—through memory. Recollection is not just a blessing. It is a lifeline to immortality. It is how we hold close the people we love but who are no longer with us. It is how, in my experience, we survive loss.

The idea that the dead exist beyond their earthly time is rooted in many cultures and traditions: In fact, outside of the West—in Latin America, in East and Southeast Asia, in Africa, in Oceanic cultures as well as in many Black traditions in the United States—ancestors are not distant names etched on a grave or in a family tree but a continued presence in the lives of the living. The relationship between the living and the dead is different from the relationship among the living, but it remains a relationship nonetheless.

In *After Life*, we witness how various people react to the tragically early death of Amber Crane. Some people who hardly knew her, like Nick Flores and Arnold King, find meaning in her death, while others, like her mother, shut themselves off from her memory, an effort to stave off pain that only increases it. But her sister Melissa's relationship with Amber continues through death, because for Melissa, the wall between life and death is more of a diaphanous veil.

Is the Amber who Melissa's been talking to all these years some sort of ghost, or a part of Amber that lives in Melissa, or something else entirely? I find the question irrelevant. What matters is that to Melissa, Amber is alive, and the love and support of a big sister survives, even grows. This love has the power to bring comfort and joy not yoked to a physical presence. Somewhere in there is a suggestion for how we might look to other traditions to better marry life and its inevitable end together.

At the same time, I write these words as the mother of daughters, young women who I love with a ferocity that sometimes takes my breath away. I can scarcely allow myself to imagine a sliver of the pain of losing them, of surviving a life taken too soon. And so, to all the mothers, fathers, siblings, relatives, and friends who have lost someone out of order, too soon, I send you all the love in my heart and I dedicate this book to you.

Gayle Forman

ACKNOWLEDGMENTS

After Life was a book that, much like Amber Crane, I thought was dead. I wrote it in 2016 and then it sat on my hard drive for six years until it was revived by Sophia M. Ramos and Suzie Townsend, who made me take a second look at this story and then delivered it into the hands of Rosemary Brosnan. So thank you to this trifecta of generous, intelligent, and hyper-competent women. The Estate of Gayle Forman is very grateful.

Thank you to the entire wonderful team at New Leaf Literary, including Pouya Shabazian, Olivia Coleman, Katherine Curtis, Joanna Volpe, Tracy Williams, and Kiefer Ludwig.

Thank you to the rest of the team at HarperCollins, including Liate Stehlik, Rich Thomas, Allison Weintraub, Tim Smith, Kathryn Silsand, Audrey Diestelkamp, Danielle McClelland, Melissa Cicchitelli, Shannon Cox, Kerry Moynagh and her sales team, Patty Rosati and her school and library team, and Jenn Corcoran, Jenny Lu, and the entire publicity team. Thank you to Agata Weirzbicka for her haunting and evocative cover illustration and to Laura Mock for the beautiful design.

Thank you to the authenticity readers: AnneMarie Clarke, Melissa-Jane Fogarty, and Samantha Tan.

Thank you to Tamara Glenny and Marjorie Ingall, who have read drafts of every book I have written. To Libba Bray and Emily Jenkins for dog walks and hot yoga and friendship.

Thank you to the readers, teachers, librarians, booksellers who have been with me now for nearly twenty years! I couldn't do what I do without you.

After Life is a love letter to family. Thank you to my family for inspiring it.